NOWHERE TO RUN

"You still wonder why I won't stay and marry Maria? And you have all the answers." Slocum stared off at the blue skies. He did not need to tell this man anything. He knew the answers.

"You killed a man?"

"The wrong one."

"But now you are in Mexico."

"Borders won't stop them. Dead or alive is not even an issue."

"Perhaps you only need a new identity."

"Tried it, even that didn't work. They still came for me."

"Like wolves." Bollinsky slapped his gloved hand with the riding crop.

"Yes, like wolves . . ."

JAKE LOGAN

SLOCUM
AND THE SENORITA

J
JOVE BOOKS, NEW YORK

This is a work of fiction. Names, characters, places, and incidents are
either the product of the author's imagination or are used fictitiously,
and any resemblance to actual persons, living or dead, business
establishments, events, or locales is entirely coincidental.

SLOCUM AND THE SENORITA

A Jove Book / published by arrangement with
the author

PRINTING HISTORY
Jove edition / November 2000

The Penguin Putnam Inc. World Wide Web site address is
http://www.penguinputnam.com

ISBN: 0-515-12956-9

A JOVE BOOK®
Jove Books are published by The Berkley Publishing Group,
a division of Penguin Putnam Inc.,
375 Hudson Street, New York, New York 10014.
JOVE and the "J" design
are trademarks belonging to Penguin Putnam Inc.

PRINTED IN THE UNITED STATES OF AMERICA

10 9 8 7 6 5 4 3 2 1

1

In the shade of the brush arbor, Montrose slapped the two fresh-cut tenderloins on the rough board table. With a dark foreboding look in his eyes, he considered the young Mexican woman. Like a cat, he reached for her, grasped her arms in his blood-encrusted fingers, and drew her slowly up on her toes to his mouth. She stifled back a scream, then seemed to accept her circumstances. A small smile began to ease into the corners of Montrose's thin lips. His mouth wasn't set for fun and laughter, but was framed in cruelty. Savagely he kissed her, and then tore his whisker-bristled lips away, holding her pressed obscenely hard against his lower body.

"Fix that meat for us to eat, then I will show you what to do next." His raucous laughter rang out across the greasewood. A wide sombrero rested on his back, and his shoulder-length dark hair, streaked with gray, was tied back with a leather string. Montrose Dulcia had returned to his hideout in the canyon. The girl shrugged off his hands and began to slice the long tube of red meat.

"I cut it from the loin of a fat heifer. It should be tender, no?" He pestered her for an answer.

The attractive olive-skinned girl of perhaps eighteen

nodded in agreement, then tried to act busy at her job. Her eyes avoided him. Montrose stalked over to the canvas pannier on the ground, drew out a brown bottle, took the cork out with his teeth, spat it away, then raised the whiskey in a salute to the others.

"To all the dumb lawmen in this territory, may they all roast their balls in hell!"

"Yeah!" came the cheer from the half-dozen men seated or squatted on their haunches on the bank of the dry wash.

Slocum sat on his own boot heels with them and studied the man. Deep in his own thoughts and considerations about this outlaw leader, Slocum used his palm to scrub the itch around his unshaven mouth. Plenty of tough men in this hideout. Montrose, the name they used to refer to the leader, was wanted in four states and territories. The biggest bounty was back in Texas—it was five hundred dollars—for Montrose dead. Lone Star officials expected delivery of his corpse or his head in a sack for their money. Mexican officials in Chihuahua offered two hundred in gold for his skull. Montrose was not only famous, but one of the most hated and feared outlaws in the Southwest.

"Hey, Pasquel, go water my horse," Montrose said, and pointed the neck of the bottle at the sweaty animal. "Bad whiskey, bah." He made a sour face to punctuate his displeasure with the taste. The young Mexican rose and hurried to obey the boss.

"You have any good whiskey, Slocum?" The man's cutting look was close to anger.

All the others glanced quickly at Slocum. The boss had spoken, and they wondered what Slocum's answer would be. However, they quickly looked away when Slocum stared at them as if to say, "What would you tell him?"

"No, I drank it all," he said flippantly.

"It must have been good. In this bottle is pure horse piss." Montrose shook the container by the neck, the desert sun reflected off the brown liquid and glass. "Who has some good whiskey?" His dark glare searched the others for an answer. One by one they began to shrug or deny any knowledge of better liquor in the camp.

"I'll have to drink this then." He turned back his head, raised the bottle by his grip on the neck, and took a great draught of the frothy brown liquor.

Slocum considered Montrose a lighted fuse, ready to explode at any moment. Over the past week, the gang leader had killed two men for frivolous reasons. Slocum's days in this deep canyon, walled in by the towering pipes of red rock that rose high overhead, had become a time of concerned apprehension for him. It was a place much easier to enter than to leave.

A bounty hunter named Shiener had dogged Slocum's trail out of El Paso and across New Mexico into the Arizona Territory. Slocum had lost the no-account around Lordsburg when he managed to send Shiener north off on a wild-goose chase up to Silver City and Mongollon while he himself rode west. After a week in the Arizona Territory, he passed through Ft. McDowell at the fork of the Salt and Verde, then headed north into Bloody Basin. Slocum had considered heading west from there and prospecting in the Bradshaws' gold district. But before he could get that far, Montrose and two of his men intercepted him.

It was mid-afternoon, and Slocum was preparing to cross the Verde River. The outlaw rode up on a stout hammerheaded horse that looked half Percheron. He reined him in and gazed down at Slocum, who'd dismounted to check his horse's shoe before fording the river.

"Not many men know this trail. Except men on the run or the law. You either?" Montrose's cold glare told Slocum that despite his Texas cow pony being between them,

Montrose might, on a simple whim, gun down a man and ask more questions later.

"I ain't the damn law."

"Didn't figure so." Montrose leaned over his saddle-horn, his hard look still as tough as when he'd ridden in. Some men like him melted when they felt it was safe; this one held that in reserve.

"I could use another man. You look like you've got lots of bottom."

"Doing what?"

"Minding your own gawdamn business. You going to ride with me or turn your toes up here?"

"That ain't the option." Slocum swung up in the saddle and reined the tough bay around. "Which way's the house?"

Montrose looked at him, smiled, and then laughed. "You're a tough sumbitch. What's the name you use?"

"Slocum."

"Gawdamn, boys, I figured he was kin to all of us, didn't you? He ain't. Our name's Smith."

"Evening, Smith," Slocum said.

"No, it ain't. Mine's Montrose Dulcia. The boys all call me by my first name."

"Montrose." Slocum nodded. He figured the other two were boys on the run. Probably got in some kind of trouble where they were raised, and stole a horse to get away, which kept them from ever going back. They looked dull-witted, a stage that most boys in their teens went through when they accepted another's leadership in place of their old man beating hell out of them. These two had traded one slave driver for another, and this one could get them hung.

"You're traveling light?" Montrose said, and reined the big swing-footed black in beside Slocum's horse.

"Hard too."

"Yeah, that pony looks gaunt." Montrose looked

thoughtfully over his outfit. "I guess we ain't never met."

"Not out here."

"Figured that sheriff up in Pres-kitt, he might of sent some spy over here dressed as an outlaw, unshaven, and have him move in my hideout, and then later he could lead a posse back up here, huh?"

"Guess he'd send a tough one."

"Yeah, about like you."

"I came from El Paso by way of Lordsburg to get here."

"You could have rode down to Hayden's Mill and circled back up here."

"Not me."

"Yeah, you sound right. Something about you, Slocum . . ." He shook his head in disapproval. "There's something familiar and I can't figure it out."

"Maybe it was prison time we did together."

Montrose laughed. "Hobby, this guy thinks he knows me from prison."

"Can't be, can it?" the blond-headed youth asked.

Slocum twisted and looked at the boy's blank face.

"Naw, mister, he ain't never been there," Hobby said.

"Shame," Slocum said, and spurred the bay to keep up with the larger horse.

"What else you do besides saw bars?" Montrose asked. He was amused at his own joke, and his belly, which hung over his belt, shook with his laughter.

"Drive cattle, deal cards."

"Banks, stages, or rustle?"

"Whatever you like." Slocum shrugged away any concern.

"See those cattle working off up this dry wash?"

"Six head, by my count." Slocum rose in the stirrups and surveyed them. "Four cows, and two big calves, one's got a slick ear."

"Yeah, you know cattle, all right. Rope that branded

heifer. We're having the back strap off her for supper tonight."

"Why not the slick?"

" 'Cause it ain't smart to eat my own cattle. They never taste as good as the other ones."

"Then why don't we brand it?"

"Won't need to. Besides, they don't recognize my brand."

"What do you use?" Slocum threaded out the riata, his slender braided rawhide lariat made by an old man's skilled hands deep in Mexico.

"Three Sevens. Wasn't that branded on Cain's forehead?"

"Damned if I know. Never knew him." Slocum set the bay up the sandy wash in a short lope. The longhorns, seeing his approach, broke and ran. The notched-ear heifer was too milk-fat to get away; she trailed the rest. He pushed the Texas pony up close enough to encircle her nodding horns and head in his loop, pitched the slack over her hip, dallied his riata, turned his horse off, and tumbled the heifer end over end. In an instant, Slocum was on the ground and had three of her legs tied with his pigging string. Bawling loudly, the heifer tried to kick free, but his tie held despite her thrashing.

"You ain't a bad hand with that gut line," Montrose said, and dismounted. "Nice damn work. I always like to watch a pro at anything."

"Bring the damn ax," Montrose said, scowling with impatience at the two boys. "You two would get caught stealing a damn cream can, you're so damn slow. Get over here. Who's got a sharp knife?

"Bow, you hit her in the head and shut up that bawling. Hobby, you split her down the back and take that strap off her."

"Not taking the hind quarters?" Slocum asked, coiling up his riata.

"No. These little ranchers around here are all chicken-shits. I been trying to get them mad enough to fight me for years. They ever do, I'll run their asses out of this country and they know I can do it."

The blond-haired boy, Hobby, soon brought Montrose the two three-foot-long strips of bloody meat. "Looks okay to me," Hobby said.

"Yeah, that new Messikin girl can cook them tonight." Montrose laid them over his lap.

Slocum tied up his lariat, then undid and recoiled the pegging string to put it in his saddlebags. The notion of his supper riding spread across the man's dirty canvas pants all afternoon didn't encourage his appetite. He didn't dare look back at the carcass—might make the man think he cared. The waste niggled him, but there was no chance to do anything else but lump it. He mounted and pushed the bay pony on.

"You like Messikin women?" Montrose asked.

"They all strike me."

"Yeah, well, a coyote brought her here for a song. She ran off from the whorehouse too many times. The madam, you may know her. Lucinda down in Nogales?"

Slocum shook his head.

"She said, the best lesson my girls can learn. You run away, I'll send your ass to Montrose and his horny out-laws."

"Sounds bad enough to me."

"Yeah. I don't pay them either." His boisterous laughter shattered the rolling brown grassland studded with junipers and century plants.

The next day in camp, Montrose told Slocum to saddle up. He did as he was ordered, and wondered what the big man was up to. They left the deep canyon confines, some-thing no one did unless Montrose said so. There were three outlaws, counting the boss. They rode north several hours to a small ranch headquarters. Nestled in a grove of cottonwood trees, the corrals were made of stacked dead poles and the house was a low-walled adobe with a shake roof.

The floor inside was obviously lower than the outside ground, as Slocum could see when a woman came to stand in the step-down doorway. She was dressed in a button-up-the-front faded calico dress, and her brown hair was uncombed. She swept it back with her hand and looked at them all with dead eyes.

"Charlie gone?" Montrose asked, dismounting and openly hitching his crotch.

"You don't see him," she said, and shrugged.

"Come on up here," Montrose said to her.

She shook her head and paled.

"I said, get your ass up here."

"No, don't make me do that—"

"Hobby, get her up here."

The boy bolted off his horse and the woman collapsed, crying, "No, no." The youth caught her by the arm and dragged her out in the brilliant sun before Montrose. She tried to hide her face and turn away, but the boy managed to hold her in his arms and drag her closer to his boss.

"Boys, get off and undress her. We need to see her bare butt." Montrose's laughter rang through the air. The other youth jumped in, and they soon stripped the dress and underwear from her slender body. Her uncovered skin was white as snow, except at her throat, face, and hands, which were sunbaked brown. She hung her head in defeat. Huddling her small breasts, she tried to make herself disappear.

"I'll handle this from here, boys. Get over there," he said, and shoved her toward a saddle slung over a low rail.

"Bend over it," he said, and roughly shoved her head forward so she was bent over the seat with her thin butt stuck up in the air.

There was no denying from where Slocum sat on his

horse that he was about to witness in broad daylight the woman's brutal rape. Montrose unbuckled his belt, undid his fly, and gave a great loud throat-clearing sound. He stepped closer, then forced her feet apart. He reached for his erection and moved in. With a roar from him and a thrust of his big butt, she cried out at his rough entry. There was nothing Slocum could do. No matter how hard it ate him up or how much it disgusted him, two pairs of eyes were locked on him. A real deputy would break under this pressure. He was being tested and he knew it.

"You want some of her," Hobby asked, the eagerness written on his face as he watched his boss's pumping actions.

"Not after the three of you." Slocum turned the bay away, tired of listening to Montrose's animals sounds and looking at his oversized hairy butt humping her.

"Where do you think you are going?" Wilton, an older outlaw, asked gruffly. Slocum realized the man had trailed them from camp—in case Slocum turned out to be a deputy.

"Going to water my damn horse, stupid," Slocum said, and gave him a look of disdain.

"Well, don't get no damn ideas about riding out."

Slocum never bothered to answer him. He booted the bay toward the large rock-walled tank of blue water. He would be glad when the others had their turns on the woman and this afternoon was over. It wasn't in his plans to be in these sorry buzzards' company much longer.

On the fourth day, they rode up the Verde. Slocum suspected it was another test. He closed his eyes as he rode. *Don't let it be that same rancher's wife.* Montrose had groused about the incident going back to camp. Why hadn't Slocum raped her too? He'd made an excuse—he never liked going last. When they turned more northwest he felt relieved for the time being. They were not headed back to the same place.

Riding up the river's course, they heard voices ahead. In a whisper Montrose told them to be quiet. Slocum had no idea what lay over the next hill, and fell behind the others.

It wasn't long until they discovered several Indians bathing in the river. From his vantage point, Slocum could see two older women with dried-up breasts and flabby bellies standing knee-deep in the stream. A girl in her late teens stood up, and the water droplets spilled off her sleek copper skin. None of the women realized they were being watched. They expected to be alone this far back in the mountains.

Slocum watched Montrose wipe the spittle from the side of his mouth with the edge of his thumb and swallow hard. His saliva was already pumping with what he expected. "I get her first, boys."

The squaws scattered all directions at their approach, but Montrose ran the girl down with his horse, snatched her by the hair, and lifted her kicking and squealing off the ground. The boys each caught them an older woman and began to rape their prizes. Slocum reined his horse around. Then a rock dislodged on the hill above him and sent a cold chill up his spine despite the hot sun. It was Wilton again.

"Better get you some of that Indian pussy," the man said, and then chuckled.

"Plenty there," Slocum said.

"Where in the hell you think you're going?"

"Get my damn horse a drink."

"I'll go with you and we can water the others. You got something against screwing Injuns?" Wilton asked as they went back up the river bottom.

"My taste in women is different."

"Yeah, well, it worries me."

Slocum looked at the man in disbelief, then laughed out loud. "Well, I gawdamn sure don't want you."

The man's face turned red and he went on by in a huff. Slocum glanced back. He wondered how far he would get, if he tried to run away. Studying the peaks that surrounded them, he realized he needed to leave this gang, but they weren't ready for him to leave. The only way out for him might be feet first.

2

Slocum reset the shoes on his bay horse. The boiling midday sun shone straight down in the narrow chasm. Hardly a breath of air stirred; the cottonwood leaves above him were still, save for the whistling of a Mexican mockingbird. Some quail called off in the greasewood. The rest of the gang members were taking a siesta. Bent over and busy reshoeing his horse, Slocum heard a soft hiss.

"Señor?"

He never looked around, and issued a soft "Yes." Then his hammer rapped in the new nail and he quickly turned up the hoof to bend the point over.

"My father is very wealthy . . ." Her voice trailed off, and he searched around to see if any of the outlaws might be awake and listening. No sign of any of them stirring. She remained on the other side of his animal. He could see her soiled skirt with the tattered hem, but no more of her.

"I thought he said you were a *puta* from the border." Slocum wondered if she was lying to him.

"I was kidnapped by bandits and sold to that wicked woman Lucinda. She was afraid I would get away and tell my father about her buying me."

12

That made sense. He drove another nail in the horse's hoof. What should he do? Hard enough for him to figure a way to escape this outfit, let alone take a girl along with him.

"I'll see what I can do. They seem wary about me," he said.

"Yes, very wary, but I won't hold you back. My name is Maria Cardinale Obregon."

"Slocum," he said. Such a name was not common for a poor *puta*, but then she could have been exposed to lots of knowledge working in that whorehouse on the border. "Maria—you be ready at a moment's notice," he hissed after her.

"Bueno, gracias."

He looked up to study her back. There was an *olla* on her head, and she started toward the spring to fill it. Obviously, she was tired of the brutal treatment at the hands of these outlaws. He'd heard her moans at night when one of them claimed her and dragged her into the brush for his own purposes. Still, survival was his game and he must not be too foolhardy and headstrong despite his true feelings of anger. Deeply engrossed in his concerns, he drove the last nail in the shoe. He straightened his stiff back and glanced across the camp. The rest of them looked asleep on their bedrolls despite the sultry heat. With a finger, he shaved the wetness from his forehead. There had to be a way to get out of this oven and their clutches.

His chore complete, he led his horse to the flats, hobbled him to graze on the short grass. A few puffy clouds began to drift over. Must be raining further north up on the Mongollon Rim, and these were tags off the afternoon thundershowers. He turned an ear and listened. A thunderstorm might throw the outlaws off guard. Not much likelihood of it reaching this far south, but any change would be a good time to make his break. When Slocum ran for it, Montrose would surely suspect he was a spy and pursue him. Taking the girl along would slow him down and provoke the man even that much more.

Slocum listened again. He could hear the far-off roll of thunder, ever so faint, a slow-rolling growl that rumbled across the land like a coarse dog's throaty sound. It was music to him. Only, instead of one horse, he needed two ready to go. That might be the largest problem. He also needed to scatter the other animals to thwart immediate pursuit. How good could the girl ride? She better be an Apache.

He could see where his rig sat on the ground among the other saddles. All their horses were hobbled and grazed close to the small spring-fed stream, which was hardly more than a trickle. It fed down the canyon to the knee-deep Verde. They'd have only one chance to try to get away. Then Montrose would be on to them. The results would turn deadly. But somewhere in the confusion of a blinding rainstorm, Slocum might manage to take her and flee. It would be chancy, but better than making a daylight run for it.

He joined her at the *olla* that she had returned with, and dipped out a drink with a gourd. They shared cautious looks. He sipped on the water, then did a quick check of the outlaws over the edge of the dipper.

"Have a sharp knife ready to cut hobbles," he said under his breath. She gave a nod to indicate she'd heard him. An attractive girl, she bore a freshly healed deep scar on her right cheek. Her brown eyes showed the weariness of her abusive captivity. He felt she knew the risk of being recaptured and the punishment it would entail.

"We may try for it if the rain comes," he said under his breath.

The slight bob of her head was enough. She understood. He went and sat with his back to a gnarled cottonwood.

From there he could observe the outlaws and sharpen the great knife in his boot.

He worked the steel edge over the stone, slowly and deliberately. His mind was set more on escape than the job at hand. Using the leather top of his boot, he stroked the large blade until it sliced the hair from the back of his hand. Returning it to its sheath in the boot's vamp, he pulled down his pants leg, then turned his attention to the jackknife in his pocket.

The first whiff of rain came on a hot wind. A sweet smell mixed with juniper and greasewood attacked his nostrils. He suppressed a grin as the older outlaw Wilton sat up and rubbed his gray-beard-stubbled face.

"Son of a bitch, it's hot," Wilton swore. "Bring me some *agua*!" he ordered Maria. Then he cast a sullen look over at Slocum. "Be quick!" he shouted.

She hurried over with a dipper and handed it to him, careful to stay back from his grasp. Wilton downed it and demanded more. His actions awoke the others. Slocum silently cursed his bad luck. Had the rain caught the outlaws asleep in the open, he and Maria might have had an opening in the confusion. There was no chance left for the plan he'd counted on. He went back to stropping the jackknife on the oil stone. There had to be a way to escape.

Soon black angry clouds raced into view and closed off the sun's light. Darkness gathered. Thunder drew closer. He pocketed the knife and ignored the outlaws' rambling talk about the approaching weather. They soon discussed putting up a canvas shelter, and it was unrolled. A rope was strung between two trees and the sheet spread over it. By then the gusts of the approaching storm were beginning to batter the cottonwoods overhead and it grew darker.

"Gather up them damn horses," Montrose said to Slocum. "A little close lightning and they might bolt away."

It could not have worked better. The horses would be picketed on a line and not hobbled. While the outlaws worked on their shelter, Slocum caught the horses, leading them back and undoing the hobbles. Black clouds rolled in, and soon rain began to pepper him. The cooler moisture felt good at first, but he knew it would soon turn into an icy chill. In his slicker, he tied the horses up as the men rushed around, shrugging on their oilskins and trying to peg down the large tent.

He found his own saddle, and wondered what to use for the girl. He took his rig behind a thick tree. Then lightning struck close by, and it left a blinding green-yellow glow with an ear-shattering spike of thunder. Slocum reached down and quickly tossed his saddle on the bay; he cinched him using the screen of the cottonwood. Then he grasped another rig. Blinded by the torrent that began to fall, he quickly cinched it down on the second animal. When he looked up in the next flash, the small form of Maria rushed from the tent to join him. He bridled both horses as streams of water came from his hat brim.

In the downpour, she paused at the tree, and then reached high as she could with a butcher knife and cut the tent rope. The large wet tarp collapsed on the outlaws. Violent curse words filled the air. No time for waiting. Slocum boosted her on the ready horse and swung up on his own. Then he began to shout above the rain in the other ponies' faces, and they all flew backwards.

"Gawdamnit, he's getting away—"

"So is she!"

With the loose horses ahead of them, she joined in his herding effort, and they swept down the canyon toward the Verde and their route to escape. Rain and wind battered them. Grave-digger bolts of lightning flashed about, startling their mounts and causing them to spook aside into the greasewood. For a moment, Slocum felt certain that his own mount would falter and fall, but the pony regained his footing and burst back beside hers.

He worried about how cold she must be without a slicker, but there was nothing he could do to help her for the moment. They needed to reach the river and cross it before the rain upstream brought it up. If they could hold the ponies together and drive them across the flooded Verde, it would slow down Montrose's pursuit even more.

In the drafts of rain that swept across the widening canyon, they pushed on. Without hesitation, the lead pony bailed off into the dingy stream, taking the others on his heels, then up the other side and south on the road Slocum had come up a week before. The horses drove well despite the deluge, and Slocum dropped them down to a trot. He shook loose his ground cloth and fashioned a hole in it to make a poncho for her.

"*Gracias,*" she said, taking it from him. With her wet hair plastered on her head, she struggled into it and nodded, pleased, once under the canvas poncho.

He twisted in the saddle with a last look into the wall of rain for any sign of the outlaws. With a toss of his head, he and Maria hurried on.

In an hour, the storm moved off and the sun reappeared. He headed up a side canyon, and hoped it would lead them to a way east into a land he was unfamiliar with. No matter, they needed distance from Montrose and his men. But by late afternoon, he found their way blocked by a blind canyon wall, and without the toeholds of a desert ram's hooves they were forced to backtrack. He allowed the loose horses to scatter. Maybe they would find enough graze in this canyon and not return to camp. Montrose never grained them much, so chances were that they would stay up here.

"What if the outlaws are back there?" she asked, returning from relieving herself in the brush. A concerned expression was written on her face.

"That's one thing we'll have to meet head-on. But I

doubt that they are that close to us on foot," he said, halfway convinced that Montrose and his men by this time were cut off by the rain-swollen Verde.

When they reached the mouth of the canyon, Slocum swung north this time. It would take them past the outlaws' river crossing, but if he and Maria were lucky, it would fool their pursuers. It amounted to a risk he felt they needed to take. Somehow they must also find food and some shelter to survive this ordeal. He hoped to keep high enough up on the mountain so the outlaws couldn't see them cut back even if they were right across the river.

He led the way, and she urged her horse after him. The game path was brushy and hardly more than a desert sheep's trail, but the mixture of juniper and mesquite stood tall enough to hide them. He rode up on the shelf at last, and then went far enough back against the face of the mountain so no one from below could see them. The going went easier, and she pulled beside him.

"Why are we going north?" she asked.

"I know Mexico is the other way. But he expects us to go south. We'll have to circle around."

She glanced back with a hard look in her brown eyes. He rose in the stirrups and studied the peaks to his right. Somewhere up there had to be a pass to cross over the mountains. He hoped the canyon they'd entered gave them such an outlet. The sun was far in the west, and he didn't dare shoot anything for them to eat. Maybe the stale dry cheese and crackers in his saddlebags would sustain them until he found them something else for their nourishment.

Soon he sent her ahead up a steep game trail in hopes of finding a way over the range. He felt his place was to guard their rear, and the pony she rode acted surefooted enough to carry her.

"This path is made for burros," she said, looking back at him.

"It's all we have." He forced a smile to reassure her. Their mounts struggled on the loose rocks underfoot, and the way led straight up, but it was not any worse than he'd expected. Most of all, he hoped it would lead them to the far side.

At sundown, they reached a small saddle between peaks, and he could see another line of trees, miles away and far below them. That must be Tonto Creek, he decided, but it was too far away for them to try to reach before darkness.

"We'll find a flatter place and stop for the night," he promised her.

"Can they find us?"

"They can find us. But I don't think so tonight."

She gave a noticeable shudder of her shoulders under the poncho and swallowed hard.

"It won't be easy," he promised her, and started down the trail on foot, leading his horse.

"I know that, Slocum. I am not complaining. You hear me?"

"Yes," he said over his shoulder, and ambled stiffly downhill on his high boot heels. This would be a test. Somewhere to the south was the town of Globe. They could catch a stage there and head for Tucson. Mexico was only another day's travel away from the old presidio. He had no idea where in Mexico she lived, but they could be there in a short while if they ever reached civilization. And if somehow they managed to escape Montrose's grasp.

He glanced back up; she was coming off the mountain fine. They needed to find a perch for themselves on this downgrade for the night. He could see the distant Mongollon Rim to the far north, a dark blue line of mountains that rose into more boiling thunderheads. He felt better than he had in days. Out from under the outlaws' control,

he made a few quick hops in his boots to find footing on
the steep downhill, and the bay came sliding after him in
a small avalanche of rocks. No room for a misstep up
here where the eagles soared.

3

They half slept a few hours on the ledge, high upon the mountainside. Huddled in each other's arms for warmth, they lay fully dressed in their soggy clothing and underneath his damp blankets. The night wind rustled hard through the juniper boughs around them. Slocum awoke several times and held the Colt close to his face. He tried to listen above the wind's murmur for any unusual sounds. By the starlight he could make out both hip-shot horses, strongly picketed with their butts turned toward the wind. Then he laid back with her warm form huddled against him and slept.

A few times during the night, her moans and cries forced him to awareness. Obviously, her treatment at the hands of her various captors had left her shaken and her dreams now turned to nightmares of the memory. He petted her, and soon both were asleep again.

When the sun formed a gray crest on the sawtooth horizon, they awoke. Famished and still groggy, he fed her the last crumbs of food from his saddlebags. In the blustery gale, on foot and leading their mounts, they resumed their cautious trek off the perilous mountainside. Slocum considered going back on top and surveying their backtrail, but he felt they were far enough ahead of the gang to have the liberty not to have to do that. The path proved sheer, and in several places his bay lost his footing, scrambled, and collided with Slocum's back. Only by fancy footwork did Slocum find a secure enough place to put his heels and, grasping the reins, manage to keep control of his animal. A look off the side at the depths beneath him made him catch his breath and reminded him how precarious his place was on the mountain's face.

At a tight place, he would glance up to warn Maria. Grim-faced, she would nod that she had seen the problem and would try to avoid it. After an hour-long trek along the steep trail, they reached flatter ground and halted to catch their breath. After a short rest, they remounted. He cast a final look at the peaks above them and hoped that Montrose had drowned back in the rain-swollen Verde.

At midday, they arrived on the level desert floor. He shot a yearling deer that bounded up in front of them. He dismounted, bled it, and then slung the carcass over the saddle and motioned for her to go on. They would reach the watercourse before long, and he planned to gut and skin it where there was water and a tree to hang it up in.

"A good idea," she agreed when he explained his plan for the deer.

They reined up at Tonto Creek a few hours later, and with his lariat, he swung the deer over a limb. She stripped the saddles from their horses and hobbled them. Out of breath, she joined him.

"I can butcher it," she offered.

"We both can do it," he said, and grinned at her.

"I wish I felt we'd lost them," she said, and rubbed her sleeveless arms. Maria's handsome face bore a concerned look. Obviously, she was not satisfied they were out of harm's way.

"They won't catch us," he said to reassure her, making

a cut down the deer's front leg to begin the skinning process.

"I'd like to feel that certain." She looked warily back at the mountain range they had crossed.

"Trust me," he said, and sliced open the other leg.

"He's a mean man and will be *muy* determined to get us."

"In two days, we should be in Globe. We can take a stage from there."

"Here, let me do that." She elbowed him aside. "If I was at home, there is a man on our ranch who could make this skin into a fine vest or soft gloves."

"Be a good man to know," he said, and helped her pull the hide down while she used her keen knife to expertly separate the membrane from the carcass. The skin soon was free, and she began to gut the deer, setting aside on a rock the liver and organs. She was no stranger to butchering. He wondered how the daughter of a rich rancher had learned such skills.

"Who were the men who kidnapped you in the first place?" he asked.

"A *bandito* called Lobo and his gang. I was on my way to Delores and they blocked the road. They shot poor Jose and Guermo; then they pistol-whipped my chaperone Señora Matatia. I was so afraid, I cringed in the coach and cried like a baby."

"What happened next?"

"This one they called Lobo, he dragged me out and grinned like he had found a rich treasure. I swore and kicked at him. Then he kissed me. Oh, his bad breath made me sick, and he squeezed my—breasts. I was not going to let him do anything else, but what could I do? He threw me over the lap of another outlaw named Paulo, and they rode off with me belly-down on his lap.

"This Paulo kept grabbing my bottom and I kept fighting his hands away. But he only laughed at me like it was some kind of game."

"Where did they take you?"

"To some cantina in the mountains. I did not know for sure where I had been taken." She made a face at him, shook her head, then continued.

"I never knew much. They tied me up in a back room and this Lobo said I must be a virgin for the buyer to pay the most money. I could tell it made the others in his gang mad that he wouldn't let them touch me, but they obeyed him."

She finished dressing the deer and stood back, her hands red with blood.

"Let's go clean up and we can cool the deer out in the stream," he said.

"Good idea," she agreed, and they went down the sandy bank. The stream was obviously swollen with the rain falling in the higher mountains. He brought the deer, cut out a tenderloin, then tied the carcass by a leg to a sturdy willow, and sunk it with several large rocks inside the cavity.

"That should keep it cool," she said, on her knees at the edge, scrubbing her hands. Then she washed the liver and the loin. He joined her at the river's edge and rubbed off the drying blood from his fingers in the cool water.

"Yes," he agreed with a smile. "And I'll build a fire and we can have some real food."

They dragged up driftwood and soon had a blaze going. Both of them sat on the ground, and she restarted her story, while the meat on a spit roasted over the flames.

"An older woman came to the back room. She made me undress and take a bath in cold water. She took my clothes away with her, and I was afraid she would not return with them. I had only a few feed sack towels." She shook her head in disapproval. "And could not cover myself with them if they came in the room. I huddled in a corner, embarrassed, freezing from the bath, and thought they would be back to butcher me. It seemed like hours went by. She returned with my clothes and they were clean. She told me to come over to her."

Maria made a disgusted face. "Then she made me to lay on this cot, and spread my legs so she could examine me. I was so embarrassed. At last, after poking and prodding me, she nodded and said I was a virgin. I could have told her that." Maria rose on her knees and fussed with the browning loin on the spit, turning it to cook more on the other side.

It must have been a tough situation for an innocent girl to be in, Slocum thought. This outlaw Lobo needed his butt kicked. Slocum looked off toward the peaks for any sign of Montrose and his men. He could see nothing. When he and Maria finished eating, he intended to move on south. In a day's ride, they could reach Globe if the larger Salt River wasn't too flooded for them to ford.

"That woman Lucinda came that night to the cantina," she began again. "She is a big woman, tall. Has a whorehouse in Nogales. You know her?"

"No, but I have heard of her."

"She pinched my breasts and poked me like a trader does a cow. She did not believe Lobo either." Maria made a face of disbelief. "I wondered who else wanted to see my butt. When that was over again, the two of them began to argue about the price for me."

" 'Where did she come from?' Lucinda demanded, and Lobo said, 'Far away.' That was a lie, but I was too embarrassed, too ashamed, to even say anything. I never spoke a word."

Slocum nodded. He understood the innocent girl's plight. The deer loin browned on the spit, and the aroma drew saliva in his mouth. He wished things were different and they had time to camp along this creek for a few days.

"She paid him a hundred pesos. Then she roughly

jerked me up by the arm and took me by coach to her place in Nogales. She told me on the way I would like being a *puta*. I would have money and jewelry and a nice room. I said I would never be one. She only smiled and said she had ways to make me become one. So that I would beg for a man to be inside me. I didn't know what she meant. I found out soon enough—she had ways.

"She drugged me with laudanum the first night and some old *generale* took my virginity. He was an old man and he took forever to get hard. I was so drugged I didn't care. But when I sobered up, I tried to run away. Her men caught me, dragged me back there, and she made this scar on my face with a razor." Her fingertip traced down her cheek, where the angry red streak remained. "She said I would be so scarred and ugly only an Indian would want me if I ever ran away again.

"Then a *vaquero* who once worked on the ranch came in there one night and he recognized me. Oh, I thought, if I was nice to him, he would go back and tell my father and I would be rescued. Instead, after he finished with me, that lying coyote told Lucinda who I was and she had a fit. She said I had lied to her. She slapped me and kicked me and I feared she would kill me.

"Then she arranged for this Gerald to bring me up here. Actually, she paid him to kill me and hide my body in the desert. I really expected for him to murder me when he took me from Nogales all bound and gagged and wrapped in a blanket. But he knew that Montrose would pay well for me, so he collected from her for killing me and from Montrose too."

"You really want to go home?" Slocum asked when she finished. He needed to know her true wishes.

"Yes." She blinked her wide brown eyes at him. "Why wouldn't I?"

"I took a girl home once in a very similar situation. It was in Mexico too. She had been abducted and raped by outlaws. Her father was so ashamed of her, he sent her away to a convent for life. I had to rescue her from there too."

"I can live with my shame. There was nothing I could do to prevent it. My father is a good man. You will see if you can take me there. He may not have much money, but he will welcome me home. He will reward you too."

"I will see you get there if you wish."

"I wish." She stood up and for the first time since he saw her, she smiled. "They will have fiesta, a big one at the hacienda. You will see."

He nodded. She rose to her feet and looked down at him. "While the meat is cooking, may I take a bath? Do we have time?"

"Go ahead, I won't look."

She made a face at him and then laughed loudly. "Maybe I want you to look. Are you married?"

"No."

"Good," she said, as if satisfied, and set out for the creek.

"There's a towel in my saddlebags and some soap," he offered.

She went to get them. He watched the meat and turned it. From the corner of his eye, he could see her undress, leaving her clothing on the bank. He observed her lithe olive figure wade out into the stream. She felt secure enough around him to do that—good, maybe the scars of her captivity would heal. He hoped so, considering all the worthless people who had abused her.

In a short while she returned dressed, looking fresh, drying her raven black hair, which tumbled in curls to her shoulders, and for the first time he saw life dancing in her brown pupils.

They ate loin and liver until they were full. Then he retrieved the carcass and cut a hind quarter off, that being all they could carry. He wrapped that portion in his slicker. While he hated the waste, there was nothing else he could do but hang the rest of the carcass in the tree.

The coyotes would feast come dark, if the ravens and buzzards left them any. He watched some of the large crowlike birds land with anticipation in a nearby mesquite tree and begin squawking to others that a feast might be at hand.

He and Maria saddled their horses, crossed the stream, which rose to mid-knee on their mounts, and rode south, reaching the muddy, wide Salt in a few hours.

"This river is so big," she said, looking disappointed at the wide spans of roiling brown water.

"There is a ferry upstream." He cast a look over his shoulders. More high clouds were building in the east and north over the distant rim. There would soon be more flow. They needed to cross and soon.

When they reached the bank opposite the ferry, he shouted to the operator on the far shore. The ropes were anchored at the edge of the water. He and Maria didn't have much time, the level was rising fast. To his chagrin, the man on the far side waved them away and shook his bearded face.

"No, we need across!" Slocum shouted to him.

"Too risky!"

"I'll double your fee!" Slocum felt their best chance to elude the outlaws was to be on the Salt's south bank.

"He's coming," she said in relief, also checking their backtrail.

No telling what the man would charge. It didn't matter, they needed to get across the swollen river. The man cranked on the rope and the barge rose and fell with the waves. When he reached their side, the whiskered operator spat in the water.

"Damn fool thing coming over here. Well, get on board. Cost you ten dollars. Pay in advance."

Slocum dug out the money and paid the man. They led

their horses on the rocking barge as it was battered by the swift current.

"Hold him tight," Slocum said to her about the horse. They stood in the center of the ferry. Angry water slapped hard at the upriver side and splashed them with spray.

The man spat again and began turning the crank. Slocum spotted it first. A dislodged, giant cottonwood, fully leafed, bobbed down the center of the river a hundred yards upstream, and headed straight for them.

"Look!" he shouted, and the man, seeing it with wide eyes, began to crank with all his effort. His turns were two-handed, and he put all he had into it. With only one crank on the reel, there was nothing Slocum could do to help him. The old man's efforts drew them to midstream. The cottonwood loomed larger and closer. It would wipe out the two rope cables when it struck them. Then they would be at the whim of the river and its savage forces— if the cottonwood didn't sink the barge when it smashed into the side of it.

"Get on your horse," he said to her. "When you dive off the front, slip back and let him swim. You cling to the horn, he'll get you to the shore."

"Can we make it?" Her face paled under her olive complexion.

"Yes, the shore is not steep along here."

"Oh, sweet Jesus save us—" the ferryman said between his efforts at the moaning crank.

The monstrous green ram came at them faster. To get tangled in the treetop would drown them. They were left with no option but to try and swim away from it.

"Hold on to the horn," he said to her, and busted the pony on the rump. Her horse bolted forward and dove into the river. Slocum watched him bob, then go to swimming with her clinging for her life to the horn. With a quick glance at the towering tree, he mounted and cross-whipped his pony with the reins. The bay never hesitated, and flew out into the churning water. In a few lengths, Slocum clung to the horse's tail and looked back to see the tree collide with the ferry cables. It threatened to capsize the barge, and the screaming operator jumped into the water. Slocum kicked with his sodden boots to help his horse.

The rope cables snapped like rifle shots. The tree twisted and the freed barge headed for Slocum and his swimming horse. He urged the pony on in the foot-high waves that swamped them. Then there was nothing to do but leave the horse and swim for himself. He dove down under the water, and the barge passed over him. He began to swim as hard as he could. The cottonwood turned broadside from the involvement with the cables. Limbs like tentacles reached for him. Wet clothes and boots soon took a toll on his stamina. He fought with aching lungs and legs that felt like anchors. Each time he reached with his arms, the cottonwood loomed closer.

He'd thought of lots of ways to die on the frontier, but to drown in a flooded river was not one of them. He swam harder when the limbs tugged at his boots. In his water-blurred vision, he could see the greasewood-and-cactus-clad shore. Damn!

4

"Slocum?" she cried, and struggled to drag him by the arm onto the rocky shoreline. "Are you all right?"

"Fine," he managed, coughing up fishy water and trying to rise on his elbows. He was soaked to the skin, and water drained from him like a sieve when he tried to get up.

"You sure you're all right?" Deep concern shone in her brown eyes when he looked up at her.

"Yeah, yeah." He waved her worries away and shook his dumb head. After more choking, he rose to his hands and knees on the new beach and tried to regain his breath. He searched around for her. She had gone after something. He looked up and down the shoreline for her. Soon she rounded the face of the hill leading both horses. Good, they still had their transportation. He closed his eyes and thanked the powers that be for their personal safety.

At last, wearily, he pushed himself up in his sodden clothing. Her wet blouse pressed to her ripe form made a pretty picture. He smiled at her.

"We look like two drowned geese," she said.

He reached over and hugged her tight. "Don't matter. You done good girl. Damn good, considering everything.

Saved our horses." He rocked back and forth on his sodden boots and clutched her form to him.

"What about the ferryman?" she asked.

"We better go see," he said, considering emptying his boots of the water sloshing around his socks. But he'd never get them back on again. He checked the cinch on the bay and mounted. He told her that he would be back, and rode downstream, scanning the rough water for any sign of the man. To the west, the mouth of the Salt River gorge loomed, and with the added water of Tonto Creek pouring into the Salt, the roar of the gorge could be heard for a good distance. He loped the bay and studied the still-floating cottonwood tree. After pushing the horse up a steep hillside, he spotted the bedraggled ferryman coming out of the water.

"Sorry about your ferry," Slocum said, dismounting and helping him to his feet.

"Hell, I'm still here to build another one." The man leaned on him and gasped in gulps.

"You want a ride back."

"Naw, that's my woman coming." He motioned toward the thickset Mexican woman running downhill, dodging around pancake cactus and cholla, with a half-dozen brown children coming behind her.

"Oh!" she cried from the rise above them, squeezing her clasped hands before her face. Then she broke off into a surge of Spanish about the Virgin Mary.

Slocum nodded to the man, then ran his fingers through his drying hair. He'd lost his hat in the river, and would have to buy a new one in Globe. Remounted, he waved to the woman who was taking care to go around the small boulders to get to her man. The children chattered and shouted, coming like a serpent train down the hillside after her.

Slocum topped the slope and saw Maria mounted on her horse. He rode down and nodded. "He made it too."

"Good. Where do we go now?"

"Globe. It's a mining town over the mountain. We can dry out in the sun riding there."

"Sure," she said with a smile.

They headed south on the wagon road, two well-worn ruts that wound through the greasewood. On their way, they passed some Mexican wood cutters and their string of burros going single file. Both men shouted in Spanish, "Hurry, Hurry," at the animals heavily loaded with sticks, but to no avail.

In late afternoon, Slocum and Maria reached the bustling mining town. On horseback, they wormed their way through the narrow winding streets crowded with teamsters hauling freight and huge ore wagons. He turned to her.

"You want to stay in a hotel, get a bath?"

"That would be nice," she agreed, busy looking with interest at all the people on the boardwalks, from the fancy-dressed women under parasols to the brazen *putas* trying to coax men into their lairs.

"I'll get us separate rooms," he said, dismounting at the stables.

"No." She frowned and shook her head in disapproval at the notion.

He looked hard at her.

"I'd feel much better close to you," she said. She dismounted, straightening her dress. He agreed with a shrug. Whatever she wished.

"You two been in a flood?" the older stable man asked, coming out of the office with his cheek full of tobacco. He spat to the side.

"Yeah, a big one. You grain them good," Slocum said.

"Be two bits apiece." The old man spat again, then wiped his mouth on the back of his gnarled hand.

"I can afford it."

"Figured so. Just wanted to warn you."

"Good. Where's a clean hotel?"

The man looked at him in disbelief. "You serious?"

"Yes."

"Only place I heard of that ain't got bedbugs in this burg is the Silver Dome Hotel, and it costs close to five dollars a night, mister."

"Guess I'll pay it. Come, Maria."

"You better wait, mister."

"What's wrong?"

"I've got a carpetbag in the office you can borrow. They won't let you in that hotel without luggage. Keeps the riffraff out, you see." The old man wrapped their reins on the rack and hobbled inside the office. He came out brushing dust off the satchel.

"Here, you have a nice stay in Globe."

"Thanks." Slocum nodded to the man and took the bag.

"Grover's my name." He spat again.

"Slocum's mine. We'll be riding on in the morning."

"Your horses will be gained and ready, Slocum."

They registered at the lobby desk, and he ordered bathwater to be brought up to the room for Maria. She clung to his arm going up the stairs. They stopped at the first landing to survey the spacious lobby and the great crystal chandeliers.

"This is a very expensive place," she said, her dark lashes lowered.

"A few hands of poker can pay for it."

"Or several cows?"

He agreed with a grin, and they went to their third-floor room. At the window, he pushed aside the velvet curtains, opened it to freshen the air, and studied the street. Globe was too bustling a place not to try his skill at some cards.

"They'll bring up a tub and hot water for you," he explained, "and then they'll come get it when you're through. I need to look around. I may be gone for several hours."

"You won't leave me here?" she asked in a small voice.

"No. We'll head for Tucson tomorrow. I'll find out about the stage schedule. You'll be home in three days." That would be faster than riding horseback there. He would need to sell their horses. There was plenty of time to decide.

She moved in close and hugged him. Then she threw her head back and looked up at him. He kissed her on the mouth and tasted her sweetness. He withdrew and considered her supple body. It could wait. He needed to scout out the town, win some money, and then—then he would seek her.

"In a few hours," he said. "I shall return and you will be rested."

"*Sí.*"

He smiled at the longing in her eyes, and shifted his Colt in the holster. He would need to disassemble and oil it later. Firearms did not swim well. Touched by her display of affection, he left the room with some regrets and hurried down the staircase. In moments, he moved into the crowd on the boardwalk. In the first haberdashery, he found a high-crowned hat to fit and bought it. A rain or two and it would take a shape more like the old one he'd lost in the river.

After a bath and shave in a barbershop, he ducked in the first cantina. It was crowded with faro players, half drunk and waving their money like fools at the dealer. A block further down the narrow winding street, he entered a plusher saloon called the Red Rooster. He eased his way to the bar, found a place, and ordered a whiskey. The man splashed it in a jigger and held out his hand for a quarter. Slocum paid him and over his drink surveyed the crowd. There were a number of poker tables in the rear of the room, with men of suits and substance seated around them. He felt certain his filthy canvas pants, collarless faded shirt, and raveled vest would hardly draw more than a raised eyebrow from any of them.

So when he finally edged over to one of the empty chairs, the looks said, "If you ain't got the money, don't sit down." He piled a respectable amount of coins and folding money from his pockets before him, and the men smiled in approval. They really looked more like sharks who grinned at a small fish when it swam by.

Slocum nodded. They gave him quick shots at their names. Bevins, looked like a banker; Thomas, a gambler; Burleson, a lawyer—he said so; and Thaddeus Pinworth, a merchant.

"Slocum's mine."

They nodded in agreement, anteed fifty cents, and the cards were dealt. Slocum drew a low pair and discarded two. The bets went around. Thomas raised a dollar. The others hesitated, but stayed. Slocum did too.

"Guess you've got three of a kind," the gambler said in disgust to Slocum. When he received nothing but a blank look in reply, the man pitched his cards in. Slocum waited for the others to challenge him, and the rest folded. He raked in the small pot, and from there on he played with their money.

The game shifted back and forth, but Slocum steadily increased his share.

"You in mining or cattle?" the lawyer finally asked when Slocum raked in another win.

"Both. Whichever makes the most money."

The men laughed, and the lawyer made an approving smirk. After an hour and a half of play, Slocum warned them he was down to playing his last hand.

"A matter of finding the little woman some new clothes," he said.

"Come by my mercantile. By damn, that way I may get some of my money back," Pinworth said with a red-faced laugh.

"I shall. Where is it?"

"Across the street. Pinworth's Mercantile."

"I'll be there in thirty minutes with her," he said, and tossed in his hand, which amounted to nothing.

He hurried back to the hotel. She opened the door quickly on his knock, and stood back, looking fresh from her bath. Her shoulder-length black curly locks showed the results of much brushing.

"Come on," he said. "My pockets are full of money and you need two new outfits. One to ride home in and one to show off in."

"What did you do?" she asked, hurrying to keep up with him down the hallway.

"I had some lucky poker and we're going to Pinworth's Mercantile and find you those clothes."

"But you have done so much for me—" she started to protest.

"Never mind," he said, and guided her through the traffic to cross the street. A small bell rang overhead when they entered the mercantile, and someone who looked like Pinworth's son came forward to greet them.

"Welcome to Pinworth's."

"Your father said this was the best store in Arizona."

"You know my father?"

"Yes, we met in a friendly poker game. Maria needs a divided riding skirt, a blouse and vest, boots, and, ah— yes, a hat."

"This way, Señora," the clerk said. At that, she managed a private wink at Slocum behind the man's back.

Slocum merely nodded with approval. She soon was dressed in a riding skirt, blouse, and vest to replace her tattered clothing. With a stylish black hat on, she sat in the chair to try on footwear. Boxes of boots were scattered over the floor, and Pinworth tried them on her for fit and look. When at last he found a pair to suit her, she came outside to show them to Slocum, who was on the porch smoking a cigar.

"This will be very expensive," she warned him.

"Never mind. Now find a dress for the fiesta," he said, and playfully shoved her back inside. "And some dog-skin shoes to wear with it."

"Dog-skin?" She stuck her head back out and frowned at him in disbelief.

"The best," he said, and laughed at her. His shoulder leaning against the porch post, he drew in the smoke from the cigar. He would make her forget all about those bastards that had kidnapped and raped her. And someday he'd even the score for her too.

She selected a fancy black dress of silk, and met him coming in. It fit her perfectly, and she looked taken aback when he nodded. "Now that's a fiesta dress."

"Yes, but so expensive," she whispered with a frown.

"Get the slippers yet?" he asked.

"Yes, and they feel so good."

"Great. Now let's go find some supper, it's getting late."

"May I wear this dress?"

"That's what we bought it for."

"Oh," she gushed, and hugged him, resting her face on his chest.

He bought himself a new pair of canvas pants and a white collarless shirt of soft cotton and a canvas vest. They swept out of Pinworth's store in their new wardrobes after he paid the man the sum of forty-two dollars. Their other purchases and their old clothing, in bundles, they returned to the hotel and put on the bed. Then they went out again and found a cafe that used tablecloths, for a meal of steak, potatoes, and green beans that the waiter assured him were fresh from a nearby farmer.

"In three days you will be home," Slocum said, looking her in the eye.

"And you must stay—"

He shook his head to cut off her words. "That is what we must talk about here and now." He reached over and grasped her forearms. The black dress made her look older. "I can't stay there. Men ride my trail. I'm wanted. There's a price on my head, Maria."

"But—"

"Even in Mexico. So I cannot stay at your father's house either."

She closed her eyes for a moment, then reopened them. "I understand, but why did you tell me this now?"

"So you will know why when I have to leave you."

"I will cherish the time we have together."

"You don't owe me anything."

"Slocum, I understand. You won't leave me tonight, will you?"

"No," he said with a smile. "Not tonight."

"Good," she said, and the waiter brought their food.

Later, when they returned to their hotel room, she asked him not to light the lamp. He agreed, and put his new hat on the dresser. When he turned around, she came into his arms. He bent over, and their lips met in a sweetness that floated them both away. She undid the buttons on his shirt and stripped it open. Her hot mouth over the skin on his chest. She drove her hard breasts into his stomach.

His fingers fumbled with the small buttons down the back of her dress. When it opened, she stepped quickly back and out of it, leaving her in a small thin chemise. She paused, then pulled it off over her head. He toed off his boots, and in the dim light from the window studied her small upturned breasts with their pointed nipples.

He undid his pants and stripped off his underwear. His guts roiled at the thought of possessing her body. They moved to the bed without words, kissing, his hand cupping her firmness. She sat on the bed, then moved to the center in haste. He put his knee on the bed and moved between her legs.

Her small hand grasped his turgid shaft and she made a sigh. With care she inserted him, and then anxiously pulled him down on top of her. His slow probes found her, and she raised her hips for more. With care, they became one, linked in a growing storm, until the bed ropes underneath them protested in groans.

Breathing became a raging gasp for both of them. Her bare heels began to drum on his butt. Their pelvic bones ground together, seeking the most pleasure, his harder thrusts reaching the very depths of her cavern, the contractions of her muscles stripping his skintight sword with each surge and withdrawal.

Then a cry from deep in her throat escaped into moans. She clutched him tight while a flush of fluid rushed from her vagina and she sank deep in a semiconscious state. He smiled down at her and braced himself over her.

Then he began to arouse her again. He leaned down and tasted her nipples until they hardened. Dreamy-eyed, she soon became aroused. Slowly, her hips started to gyrate to his stiff intrusion, and the contractions inside grew tighter. She moaned and tossed her head with his growing need to be at the very bottom of her palace of pleasure. He grew larger inside her, and she sucked in her breath when he finally exploded. Spent and exhausted, they melted into an embrace and slept.

In the predawn, Slocum hurried through the streets to the livery. He needed to sell the horses, buy stage tickets for their passage to Tucson. He found the livery man drinking coffee in his office, and the man quickly agreed to purchase the animals. A boy in his teens was hired to take Slocum's two saddles to the stage office. He paid the youth a quarter, which produced a big grin. Slocum left and went uphill to the Globe-Tucson stage line office with the boy on his heels, carrying the first rig on his shoulder and anxious to show Slocum how quickly he worked.

Slocum reached the stage office, and noticed a familiar horse going up the street. The rider turned a corner and disappeared. It was one of Montrose's men, Hobby. Damn, how had he gotten there so quickly? Slocum looked around, but saw nothing else familiar. He purchased two tickets for the ten A.M. departure. Checking the street, he hurried back to the hotel.

"They're in Globe," he said to her, and studied the street below from the window. "I saw Hobby down there a while ago."

"Oh, no."

"It isn't the end of the world. We can stay out of sight, slip on the stage in a few hours, and get out of here."

"Do you think so?" Worry lines wrinkled her smooth brow.

"They won't get you. I know how to do such things."

She rushed over and hugged him. "I am afraid, Slocum."

"No need, girl. We can outwit them. Here are the tickets. Regardless of what happens, you get on that stage and get to Tucson."

"But what about you?"

"I'll join you later if I have any problem. The stage leaves at ten A.M. and you be on it. Both our saddles are on the stage. Can you get these clothes there?"

"I have the carpetbag—"

"I paid the old man for it. Use it to carry our things. But be sure you're on that stage."

"I understand." Possessively, she hugged his waist. "I am afraid for you," she said into his chest. "Please be careful?"

"I will. But there are a few things I must do first." He removed her from the hug, held her out by the shoulders, kissed her on the mouth, then headed for the door. Damn, it was hard to leave such a woman. He tipped his hat and went out in the hallway. With each flight of stairs, he recalled the response of her ripe body in the bed the night before. He shook his head to try and clear it. In moments he stood in the busy street.

Which direction had Hobby gone? Slocum headed up the crowded sidewalk. In front of the first cantina, there was no sign at the hitch rack of the black horse the boy had come in on. Was he the only one of the outlaws to get a mount? Or was he scouting ahead for Montrose? The outlaw chief might not dare risk coming into the town and being recognized.

Slocum passed an obvious lawman in a black frock coat on the sidewalk. An idea came to him. But first he must locate Hobby. What was the kid's last name? He'd heard it once or twice. Slocum hurried on, coming to a large saloon called the Silver Slipper. The black stood hip-shot at the rack in the early morning sun. Hobby must be inside tanking up, either on food or whiskey or both.

The other horses at the hitch rail did not look familiar. No telling. Slocum went around back and came up the alley. He found a bar girl in the alley smoking a cigarette. Dressed only in a white shift, she avoided looking at him.

"Hey," he said with a smile.

"Hey yourself," she said, and looked away with a scowl of contempt.

"A friend of mine is in there." He removed five dollars from his pocket. "I'd like to play a trick on him. I want you to go in there and rub yourself all over him until he blows up." He waved the five-dollar bill before her eyes.

"Do what?" She frowned at him.

"I want to play a trick on this friend of mine. You go in there and work him all over. I want him so excited he blows up, but not too fast," he cautioned her.

"For how much?"

"Ten dollars if you do a good job and don't tell him I put you up to it."

She choked on the smoke and coughed. "For that much I could seduce the Baptist preacher. Tell me again what you want done."

"I want him hotter than a pistol, and don't offer to take him back to your crib, understand?"

"Oh, I won't. I mean, unless I, well—"

"No, don't take him back there. I'll come in there about ten o'clock and tell him that we have to go."

She turned her head sideways to look at him. "All I've got to do is keep him hot till ten o'clock and I earn the ten bucks?"

"You have a deal. Here's five. You get the rest at ten, when I walk in."

"Gawdamn, I'll sure be looking for you. Who is your friend?"

"The blond-headed one that calls himself Hobby. He's in there."

"Hobby, blond-headed. I'll do it." She flipped away her roll-your-own and scooped the short hair back from her face. "He'll be hotter than the Fourth of July when you get there."

"Until ten," Slocum said, and smiled at her. He watched her hurry inside with the five clutched in her hand. Five was enough for her. Why, she'd have bedded him for a dollar.

Slocum glanced inside a bank's open door to check a clock on the wall. Nine-fifteen. He made his way toward the town hall, keeping back under the porches and watching for any more signs of the other gang members or their familiar horses. He saw nothing.

At twenty till ten on the hall clock, he entered the city law office. A balding man was busy sorting papers at a rolltop desk, and looked up mildly at Slocum.

"Can I help you?"

"Yes, you the chief of police?"

"Head marshal, Andrew Swazy." The man rose and came to the counter.

"Marshal, there is a Texas outlaw by the name of Hobby Starr in the Silver Slipper Saloon. I come from that county, and the reward is two hundred on him dead or alive. He's up there at the Slipper right now."

"Two-hundred-dollar reward for him?"

"Two hundred, yes, sir, Sheriff Ben Davis of Green County, Texas, will sure pay you." Slocum wondered if the man knew anyone or anything about the Lone Star state. He hoped his story would work.

"What town is he at?"

"Greenville, Texas."

"Who's this outlaw again?"

"Hobby Starr. I don't know what he calls himself now."

"In the Slipper, huh?" The man looked deeply engrossed in thought. "Is he tough?"

Slocum shrugged. "A big blond-headed kid, you can't miss him."

"Your name?"

"Alan Thorpe. I don't care what you do about him. My stage is leaving in a few minutes." He motioned to the schoolhouse clock on the wall. "But that's Starr, all right."

"You've done a citizen's good deed, Mr. Thorpe," Swazy said, and took down a sawed-off shotgun from the rack. "Have a safe trip. I'll go arrest this Starr."

"Good day," Slocum said, and left the office. He kept an eye out for any of the others as he hurried through the traffic and reached the stage office. The driver was seated on the box ready to leave. The man behind the handlebar mustache scowled down at him with his hands full of lines. "About time you got here. Damn near left you behind."

With a wave to him, Slocum climbed in, closed the door, and grinned at Maria. She looked pale and concerned, but somewhat relieved at his appearance. The driver's action sent the horses charging off on their way, throwing him onto the seat beside her. They were alone.

Slocum turned and looked out the side window as he settled in place next to her. He glimpsed the determined-looking, balding lawman heading up the boardwalk, armed with the short shotgun, as the coach shot past him racing through the narrow street, scattering everyone back at the driver's shouting and the fresh horses' charge. Slocum bent over and tasted Maria's sweet lips. Her arms encircled his neck.

"I was so worried you would miss the stage," she said, and kissed him again.

"I had to arrange for his arrest."

"Whose arrest?"

"Hobby's," he said, and began to laugh. Then he squeezed her chin between his fingers and gazed into her liquid brown eyes. They would be in Tucson by ten that night. Then the trip to Mexico, and he could deliver her home. He settled back with her in his arms. In three days, not over four, they should be at her father's ranch. It would be a nice way to live, to wake up with her in his bed every morning. He closed his eyes. Better savor the honey while he could. The flowers would soon wilt in his world and he'd be making a dry camp in some lonely canyon with a pack of coyotes for his soulmates.

5

Tucson's daytime heat had begun to evaporate under the twinkling stars. The coach rushed up the narrow streets, scattering cur dogs and parting the city's commerce like waves in a clipper ship's wake. The continuous adobe buildings along the street's course formed a prisonlike wall, with only an occasional light in a window or doorway. Then, with a loud "Whoa!" the driver drew up in front of the Congress Hotel.

Chinese lanterns decked the porch, and Slocum stepped down into the ovenlike temperatures. Maria followed, and he took the carpetbag from the driver.

"Any problems, Charlie?" the agent asked, coming out on the boardwalk.

"Uneventful," the driver said, handing down a small strongbox.

Slocum waited for the man to hand down both saddles.

"You two having a honeymoon?" the driver whispered. Slocum nodded.

"Whew, lucky man. Good luck to both of you," he said, sounding impressed. "Got two bags of mail too," he shouted to the agent.

Slocum escorted Maria to the lobby and had a bellboy

take their gear inside. He got them a room, and they went up to the second floor. When they entered the room, he was grateful that someone earlier had opened both windows. A cooler breeze rippled through their corner room.

"Where will you go next?" she asked, letting the night air sweep her face at the window.

"Kind of wherever the whim takes me."

"Will you stay at our hacienda long?"

"What would it do for your honor?" He stood behind her, and she laid the back of her head on him.

"I am not a virgin."

"Still, you must have a life to live when I leave."

"It is not fair—"

He kissed her. Arguing wasn't called for. He swept her up in his arms and carried her to the bed. Why waste such a wonderful night and a clean bed? He toed off his boots.

The rooster crowed and they climbed aboard the Nogales stage. In minutes they were southbound in the rocking coach. The cool air and dust filtered in the windows as they sped toward the border. At mid-afternoon they would be at the border. He studied the gray saguaro-studded land, knowing she would soon be slipping from him.

"Is there a stage to Delores?" he asked.

"Yes, we can be there tomorrow."

"How far is the hacienda?"

"A half day's ride from there."

"What will your father say?" he asked idly, slouched down beside her in the front seat, rocking back and forth to the stage's motion. Her father might respect a rescuer, but not a lover.

" 'My baby, thank God that you are alive.' "

"Good," he said, satisfied.

Road-weary and groggy from a lack of sleep, they arrived in Delores the next day. He rented a buckboard at a livery, then loaded their saddles and bag in the back and helped her on the seat. The heat of the day shone hard on them. He clucked to the team, swung them around, and under her guidance left the fortresslike village. They took the well-used road east through the tall cactus and sun-cured grass. In a few hours they reached the hills, and the vegetation changed to live oak, stolon, and juniper.

A fresh breeze swept his sweaty face, and he drew the horses up to breathe.

"How much further?"

"Two hours," she said, and nuzzled her face against his sleeve. "It will be hard for me not to show my affection for you."

"You will have to become the proper lady again."

She rubbed her legs under the riding skirt with her palms. Then numbly, she nodded. "It still will not be easy."

He laughed and clucked to the team. They stepped out in a long trot, and he hugged her to his side. "Won't be easy for me either," he said.

They reached the top of the pass. Below, the green fields and orchards of her family's place sprawled down the stream-fed valley. He was impressed by the operation. He reined the horses to a walk going down the grade.

"Pretty place," he said, and turned at her sniffles. She was crying, and there was not much he could do for her. Sadness at her return, or just the realization of her kid-napping and abuse, had finally overcome her.

"Oh, I never thought I would see it again—"

"I understand," he said. They reached the first vineyards on the hillsides, so well cared for and manicured. Two men armed with rifles stepped out in the road.

"Who are they?" Slocum asked, reining in the team.

"What is wrong, Juan?" she asked, wiping tears.

"Señorita Maria?" the man shouted, and both of them ran forward to see if it was her.

"What is wrong?" she asked.

"*Banditos.* They have struck twice since they took you."

"My father—"

"Oh, it is only a scratch."

She whirled to Slocum with a look of shock and said, "We must get to the house at once." He nodded to the men, and clucked to the team.

"Good to see you. Glad you are fine!" the men shouted after them.

"Oh, what has happened here?" she asked, her hand on his arm as he hurried the team for the headquarters. There were excited shouts from others in the fields who recognized her when she passed them, and they fell into a run in the buckboard's dusty wake.

Slocum swung the team through the portal and made a half circle, sawing on the bits to stop at the front entrance to the sprawling two-story house. A tall man with his arm in a sling came from the front door, shouting her name. She bailed off before Slocum completely stopped, caught herself, and then ran pell-mell for him. They collided in a hug and began babbling in Spanish.

"Daddy, this man saved me. His name is Slocum." She dragged her father to the rig and the two men shook hands.

"Don Miguel—call me Miguel. I never thought I would see her again," her father said in flush-faced amazement. "I owe you so much for bringing her back."

"Who hurt you?" Slocum asked, motioning to his injured left arm.

"Bandits. They are ruling northern Mexico."

"Are there many of them?"

"Maybe a dozen, twenty, who knows." A look of disgusted dismay on the man's face told Slocum enough.

"Who is leading them?" she asked.

"Lobo," Don Miguel said.

"He's the one who kidnapped me."

"Really? That *bastardo*!"

Slocum looked around. Two of Don Miguel's men had taken the hot team and unhitched them. Slocum nodded his approval, and followed Maria and her father inside the great house. It was cooler there in the hills than lower down in the desert at Delores. As Slocum removed his hat, he observed that the interior showed much craftsmanship. It was obviously built by men of skill. The two great oak front doors were carved with religious figures like a church. Tile floors stretched throughout the house.

"Forgive me for being such a poor host—but to have my Maria back," Don Miguel said. "I am a widower and my Maria is all I have in this world."

"Hey, I understand," Slocum said, admiring the room's cut-glass chandelier.

With the tired-looking Maria tucked under his good arm, the don ordered wine and food from his housekeeper, and showed them to the large table.

"Everyone told me you were dead." Miguel's shoulder shuddered as he stood above her.

"The man didn't kill me as he was supposed to. He sold me to an outlaw called Montrose up in Arizona. Slocum saved me from him."

"What can I pay you?" he asked Slocum.

Slocum shook his head. "I will accept your hospitality for a short while and that will be enough."

"But can't I—"

"No."

"Father, I will explain. Let him eat, then clean up. We both could probably sleep for days."

"I will do as you wish, my daughter."

Slocum nodded, and the rich-smelling food began to arrive. He drank of the red wine and nodded his approval, knowing it was a product of the ranch. When Slocum was at last full of food and drink, his host showed him to a spacious bedroom with a thick feather mattress on a huge bed for his personal use. Slocum undressed and fell asleep facedown.

He awoke to the sounds of shots, like Chinese firecrackers bursting in his ears. He fought his way from the depths of hard slumber. Colt in his fist and barefooted, he threaded the dark tiled floors of the hallway. A few lighted candles guided his way.

What in the hell was happening? A raid by bandits? He peered across the dark great room and could see the front door was open.

In a second, the door opening filled with someone wearing ammunition belts; Slocum dropped to one knee. The invader opened fire with his hands pouring orange red flames out the muzzle of two revolvers. Slocum's bullet to the outlaw's chest slammed him out the door. Satisfied the invader was down hard, Slocum rose and raced across the room to be certain that the man was out of commission. Then a bullet struck the door facing over his head and showered him with splinters.

He returned fire at the rider, but the bandit already was spurring his horse for the gate in the starlight. The invader lying on his back on the porch did not move. Slocum took the revolvers from his limp hands as a precaution.

"Where is my father?" Maria cried, rushing out the door to hug him.

"I don't know." He stuck the guns in his waistband, then tucked her under his arm to comfort her.

"Señorita, come quick," someone shouted, and waved for her to follow him.

"Oh, no—" She broke away and ran after the man. Slocum was close on her heels.

They found the *patrón* on his back, his head in the lap of one of his men. A woman held up a candle. The blood-soaked white nightshirt told Slocum Maria's father had taken several bullets. Damn, it hurt him to see her on her knees, hugging his lifeless body. Slocum looked to the star-flecked sky for some help.

6

Don Miguel's funeral filled the small community of workers and their families with deep sadness. Several government officials came from Delores and promised Maria there would be much action by the *rurales* against his murderers. A tall, impeccably uniformed Captain Igor Bollinsky spoke to Slocum after the services.

"They go and hide in the confines of the Sierra Madras," Bollinsky began. "No one can find them up there. It is the same story each time we try to follow them." The man's English was so impeccable, Slocum wondered more about his background than his excuses for the lack of law enforcement.

"Tough mountains. I was in them with Crook's scouts," Slocum said.

"Apaches?" The man's clear blue eyes narrowed as if he was taken aback.

"Chiricahuas."

"Yes. You were at their strongholds?"

Slocum nodded.

"There are still some of them up there in those peaks," said the captain.

"I understood that they all didn't surrender," replied Slocum.

"The matter of this Lobo, the bandit—I would like to put him under arrest. Could you lead me in there where he hides?"

"It's been a few years." Slocum dropped his head. "No, I couldn't lead you in there. An Apache took me when I went back in there. It is complicated. You can get all tangled up, and it's an easy place to fall off a mountain."

"Very well, I understand. You have no motive to send yourself to the hells up there. I must say that your recovery of Maria from her kidnappers was certainly commendable." Bollinsky snapped to attention, saluted Slocum, and excused himself. He paused a few feet away, and turned back.

"If I found an Apache to lead us in there, would you go back up there and help me find them?"

"Lobo and his bandits?"

"Yes. You sound as though you would have reservations about going after the remaining Apaches." A mild look spread over the captain's hard chiseled face.

Slocum nodded and let it go at that. The Mexicans would either execute or imprison the last Apaches if they managed to find them. Slocum had no heart for such an ending. Their days as a people were over anyway. Geronimo was somewhere in a Florida prison, along with all the army scouts who'd brought him in. Slocum felt no need on his part to search out the last tribesmen and eradicate them. The Chiricahuas were a lot like him—homeless and hounded to the ends of hell. The bandits were a different story—he owed them for Maria's suffering and Don Miguel's death.

When everyone left and at last Slocum and Maria were alone in the mansion, they sat under wavering candlelight at the great table.

"What did the captain want from you today?" she asked.

"He thinks your father's killer and the kidnapper Lobo are hiding in the Sierra Madras. He asked if I would go and help him find them."

"What did you tell him?"

"It hinges on him finding an Apache scout to lead us in there."

She blinked her bloodshot eyes, questioning him.

He raised the goblet of wine. "I'm not leaving you right now."

"Good. Will you stay for a while?"

"As long as I can."

"Will you sleep with me?" she asked in a small voice.

"Will it help or make it worse later?" He set the glass down on the table.

"For now, it will help me very much." She bolted up from her chair and came to sit on his lap. He cuddled her, and she wept until her tears soaked through his shirt.

The next day, Slocum began to reorganize the hacienda's defenses. At dusk each day, two wagons were placed in the portals to block the entrance to the yard. Away from the main house, men went in armed pairs to do their chores in the fields. The main *segundo* was a short bow-legged man in his fifties called Franco. His brown eyes held the strictness of an officer.

Together, Franco and Slocum examined the strong and weak points of their defenses. There were signal fires ready to light at various places in case the bandits returned. More wild horses were captured, brought in, and broken to replace the ones stolen by the bandits. To Slocum, the outlaws' main purpose in their raids was to steal riding stock, and that was all they'd managed to get away with, besides murdering the don.

Franco worried about the cattle in the hills being stolen by border bandits while this new remuda was being broken to ride. Slocum rode some long loops with him to check on them. They found good numbers of the cattle, and Slocum was convinced the herd had not suffered many losses.

"I plan to hold a roundup and drive the fattest three-year-old steers to Delores and sell them," Franco explained. "Don Miguel said he needed to have a good sale this fall."

"We can do that," Slocum agreed. "When we get enough horses broke to ride and men ready. Maybe we should hire some *vaqueros* for that purpose. I'd hate to leave the place unguarded."

"Good idea," Franco agreed as they rode into the hacienda after a long day's ride.

"You two find anything interesting?" Maria asked from the porch.

"No."

"Supper is ready for you. And Franco, I bet your wife is looking for you."

"Ah, *sí*," he said, and laughed.

A boy took Slocum's horse and he thanked him. Maria waited with a look of impatience in the doorway. He came up the stairs with a smile for her.

"You were gone so long today," she scolded.

"Ranch business. We're going to gather some steers soon and drive them into Delores and sell them."

"What if the *banditos* learn and try to take them from you?"

"They better come armed."

"Oh, Slocum—if I lost you—"

Inside the security of the house, he bent over and kissed her. All day riding in the hills he had thought about her supple body and taking her to bed that night. He swept her up in his arms.

"But there is supper," she protested.

"Who cares?"

"Aren't you hungry?"

"For you."

She hugged his neck and shook her head. "What will the kitchen help think?"

"If they don't know already, they never will." Excited at the prospect of their lovemaking, he carried her lithe body in his arms down the hall to their bed. Someone began knocking at the front door. He stopped with a wry look of disgust. Who in the hell was there? She struggled to be set down. Reluctantly, he put her on her feet.

"Who is it?" He could not see who it was, but could hear Mona, the chief housekeeper, talking in Spanish to someone.

"Captain Bollinsky," Maria whispered, straightening her dress and fussing with it to be sure she looked presentable.

"We better feed him," Slocum said, disappointed, and followed her back down the hallway. His gaze followed her shapely butt—damn fine time for the captain to show up. He drew in a deep breath—oh, well, they would do it later.

"Captain," she said in greeting. "What brings you out here?"

The man nodded to both of them and gave Mona his stiff-brimmed hat. "Business, I fear. I came to see if Señor Slocum would ride with me to the mountains."

"Supper is on the table and we were about to eat. I am sure the two of you can discuss this over food."

"You've found a guide?" Slocum asked.

"Oh, yes. Raphael Leyba is a full-blood Apache. He is married to a Mexican woman and they have a farm in a small community near my post. He has been to the mountains many times."

"How many men will you take?"

"Ten."

"Have a seat. There will be time to discuss this later,"

Maria said, and poured them goblets of wine, indicating a place on each side of her chair.

"Ah, I must have timed my arrival perfectly to impose on you for supper," Bollinsky said to her.

"Perfectly," she said.

Slocum, busy filling his plate, thought the same thing. The man had also arrived in the middle of his passionate plans for Maria. He wondered what caliber of men rode with this officer. Even with an Apache guide, he didn't feel comfortable going in there with cutthroats from prison recruited to be *rurales*. Many Mexico conscripts in uniform came from such populations.

"These ten men?" Slocum asked quietly, glancing up at the officer.

"They are career military men."

"You trust them with your life?"

"Absolutely. You have any concern?"

"I've been in those mountains with Apache scouts. They would have laid down their lives for me. A few times they almost had to."

"I have carefully weighed the perils of this undertaking. The men I've selected are not shiftless, nor without courage, and have performed under fire before. I completely understand your concern, Slocum."

"Good," Slocum said, and went on slicing the browned hunk of steak on his platter.

"Is it safe even going in there?" she asked.

Bollinsky looked at her over the rim of his wine glass. "Nothing in this state is safe as long as those bandits can swoop down and kill property owners and kidnap innocent people."

"I agree with that. When will you leave?" she asked.

"If Slocum can leave—in the morning." He gave both of them a quizzical look.

"Oh, so soon," she said in a little voice.

"It would be better not to talk about it and just do it,"

Slocum said. "Then the bandits can't be warned of our coming and be ready for us."

"Exactly my thoughts," Bollinsky agreed.

"What will you need?" she asked Slocum.

"My horse, a bedroll."

"We have provisions," Bollinsky assured her.

She nodded that she understood.

Later that night in her bed, after their fiery lovemaking, Maria cuddled in Slocum's arms. Her silky, firm body nestled against him. Her fingers fussed with his hair.

"You will be careful in those mountains. I would so hate to lose you."

"I promise to be careful. Don't leave the ranch. I figure sooner or later that Montrose is coming after the two of us. The ranch guards can handle him and his bunch. But don't you take any chances." He drew a deep breath. "When I return, if he persists, I will deal with him."

"But how—"

"I'll cross that bridge when I come to it."

Her palm rubbed over his flat lower stomach, and soon her attentions began to arouse him. She quickly rose and straddled his legs. Her hand, pumping up and down the shaft, quickly restored more life to his manhood. In a swift move, she rose and leaned forward until she buried his throbbing shaft in her slick void.

Starlight filtered through the open window into the room, giving him a grand picture of her naked form. She began to ride him in a willowy dance with her hands held high over her head. Her small pointed breasts jiggled with her every movement, and she gave him a mischievous grin. He closed his eyes to savor the pleasure. In the morning he must leave her and ride off with the captain. Was this the right thing for him to do? She began to contract with spasms inside, and he lost all thought about the future. He pulled her down and took the hard knob of her left nipple into his mouth. The world swirled around them.

7

In the golden early morning light, Slocum could twist in the saddle, look back, and still see the green orchards, fields, and vineyard. They rode into the foothills in a column. Ten mules followed, heavily loaded with supplies and bedding. The captain's first noncom was a big man named Sergeant Angelo. He wore a great mustache and looked like a grizzly bear in size. His voice too reminded one of a bruin, Slocum decided, but Angelo demanded attention from his men and received it.

Maria's sweetness still flavored his mouth, and the flowery-smelling musk of her body lingered in his nose. He was grateful for the time away from her so he could get used to the idea and ease himself away from the enticing memory of her muscular body. He would have plenty of time to think about the bandits and the mountains ahead. Earlier, he'd met their Apache tracker and the man had remembered him.

"You and Tom Horn big friends," the Apache had said.

"Yes. Who did you ride with?"

"Juh. When he died, I went to live with my woman's people. I did not like the one they called Geronimo."

"Juh fell off his horse into a river?" Slocum asked.

"He was not drunk," the Apache said sharply.

"Some think his heart quit." Slocum recalled the rumors that flew around San Carlos and the other posts when they learned back in Arizona that the main Apache war chief had fallen dead. Many knowledgeable men in the command feared Juh worse than any of the other Apache leaders. His skilled attacks had killed several soldiers, including a well-liked captain and his unit in the Whetstones. The officer's name escaped Slocum at the moment.

"Juh was not shot nor was he drunk," the Apache repeated.

Slocum agreed, and told the man he was pleased to be going to the mother mountains with him. In his *peon* clothing and straw hat, Raphael hardly looked different than the rest of the common population. For a Chiricahua, he had assimilated well into the ways of his wife's people. However, when he leaped on his horse, any reservations about whether the man was or wasn't an Apache were gone. The tribesman had a certain leap that Slocum recalled very well from his scouting days. Raphael might have dressed like a Mexican, but he unmistakably mounted a horse like a Chiricahua warrior.

"Where do you think these bandits are hiding?" Slocum asked Bollinsky during a break they took at midday to rest the horses and mules that had been pushed hard all morning.

"Above the Rio Blanco. I have some good reports they have a *rancheria* there that they use as their headquarters."

Slocum nodded. "There are people living in those mountains who may owe an allegiance to this man Lobo."

"I know that. We must be swift before they can warn him that we are coming." The man looked around to be certain they were alone. "When this is over, will you marry her?" Bollinsky asked quietly.

"Maria?"

"Yes."

Slocum looked back in the direction of the hacienda, which was obscured by the roll of the hills. The man's words knifed him in the gut. He would if he could. The reality of his situation kicked him hard in the crotch, and he straightened his shoulders. With a slow shake of his head, he fought the knot behind his tongue. "No."

"I only wondered," said the captain.

The second day, they reached the foothills. Raphael scouted the way ahead and left signs for them to follow. The towering peaks, painted in a hue of hazy purple, rose into the sky like a great wall from north to south. Slocum wiped his sweaty face on his sleeve. He was anxious to reach the higher elevations and the cooler temperatures. The canyon they rode through trapped the midday heat in ovenlike fashion. Fluffy clouds began to gather, and he realized afternoon showers would soon dampen parts of the range.

Only a few tough plants clung tenaciously to the gravelly soil on the canyon's floor, scoured by many flash floods that swept through the narrow chasm. The clack of their horses' shoes echoed in the confines. High above, a few buzzards lazily floated on the updrafts. Slocum wondered if the birds of carrion knew anything that he didn't about the future. Then he guided his horse around a head-high boulder.

They reached the base of the narrow trail, and Slocum looked up apprehensively at the mountain face. It was hardly more than a goat path. His inside boot and stirrup scraped on the rock face. His other boot hung over open air as his mount pushed forward. No room for a mistake or an ambush. He wiped his wet upper lip and tried to concentrate on the route toward the azure sky. The bare rock proved slick and horses slipped, causing the others to stop. In the rear a jackass brayed in protest at something. Slocum did not bother to look back. He patted his horse on the neck and reassured him when they started again. It was no place to panic. The distance to the rock debris below was hundreds of feet. He switched reins and dried his palm on his pants. One thing for certain. He wanted to be up on top and off this ledge to hell.

The trail offered no letup when he rounded the next corner behind the soldier's horse ahead. All he could see was more narrow pathway going skyward along the face. The private behind him muttered prayers to a chorus of mule honking. Neither sounds eased Slocum's concerns, nor indicated how far it was to the end of the trail, which he felt must be around still another bend of this slender ribbon.

The sun's rays, reflected off the wall beside them, raised the temperature until his horse dripped in sweat. Nodding his head and blowing each time during a delay, the animal paused patiently, and then set out again when the line began to move. It would be good to let the horse stop and really get a chance to blow. They had been on the steep march for a long time. Then Slocum heard someone shout in Spanish, "We are there."

The gelding even acted grateful, making the last long steps to put them on the flat. Slocum dropped to the ground on weak legs, and grasped the saddlehorn until they stiffened enough to support him. He looked around at the scrubby pine while the weary animals gave snorts of relief in the dust.

"There is a spring south of here," Bollinsky said, walking over to him. "We can rest there. My men are going to lead their horses up there."

"Good idea. Mine's about spent."

"And you have a good horse," the officer said in his haughty way.

Slocum wasn't offended by the man's words. It was his officer's training in Europe that no doubt gave him such airs. He'd known others like the captain—they never let their guard down. Officer first, man second.

"Lead the way," Slocum said, and wanted to add, *An enlisted man will lead yours for you.* But he saved the comment, and watched the knee-high once-polished boots strike off in a southerly direction, making little puffs of dirt when Bollinsky's heels struck the ground. There was nothing like the military. Slocum shook his head and started after the man.

In a short while, the soldiers' and animals' thirst was quenched by the cool water. The troopers spilled on the ground, taking siestas in the shade. Two enlisted men cooked over very small guarded fires. Slocum sat on his haunches and smoked a small cigar.

"You are a man of many talents," Bollinsky said, standing above him with a riding crop in his hand.

"And a master of none," Slocum added.

"You saved Maria from another band of outlaws, she says. Tough ones in Arizona."

Slocum nodded.

"Then you were willing to chase down the man who kidnapped her and sold her to some whorehouse in Nogales."

"Lobo most likely killed her father."

"Yes. But you say you will not stay with her. I only wonder why you do all this then."

"Maria is a good woman. She is a friend. Wouldn't you do such for a friend?"

"No. This is my duty."

"We're different then."

"No. We are more alike than anyone on this mountain. You have been an officer."

"Yes, but that was years ago."

"You are educated."

"You still wonder why I won't stay and marry her? And you have all the answers." Slocum stared off at the blue skies. He did not need to tell this man anything. He knew the answers.

"You killed a man?"

"The wrong one."

"But now you are in Mexico."

"Borders won't stop them. Dead or alive is not even an issue."

"Perhaps you only need a new identity."

"Tried it, even that did not work. They still came to me."

"Like wolves." Bollinsky slapped his gloved hand with the riding crop.

"Yes, like wolves." Slocum rose stiffly to stand up. He had seen the scout coming through the timber. "The Apache is back. Maybe he has some news."

"Yes." They both started forward to meet the man, and he bounded off his horse when close to them.

"Lobo is at the *rancheria*."

"Good," the captain said, sounding pleased. "How far away?"

"A half day's ride."

"How many men are there?"

"Maybe a dozen."

"Good. Can we go in the darkness?"

The Apache hesitated, then agreed.

"Good, at daybreak we will charge them."

Slocum nodded. Somehow he had not expected it to be this easy. Lobo was not a stupid outlaw. He had escaped the *federales* and others in the past. Maria had told him that Bollinsky was famous for running criminals into the ground. Were they lucky, or would the task be harder than it sounded? They would know when the sun came over from the gulf side of the Madras.

That evening, with his belly full of half-cooked frijoles, Slocum cinched up the rested bay and studied the starry sky. No more signs of any thundershowers. He wondered how soon the rains would return to the high country. It was the monsoon season, and about every afternoon somewhere in the range they built up. None had fallen for them that day. Already the night's temperatures had begun to drop, and he knew he would need to wear his jumper before dawn. They left two men in camp with the noisy mules and supplies. Everyone else armed with repeaters and handguns, mounted up and began the trek for the hideout.

Past midnight they dismounted and secured their horses. Then, on foot like fleeting shadows, they swept through the darkness under the tall pines and over a high ridge to descend into the valley of the outlaws' *rancheria*. Spread out, they advanced stealthily. Men moved wider apart to encircle the hovels that Slocum could make out along the gurgling stream.

When a dog yapped, they stopped, held their breaths, and let him calm down. Then, with the sergeant's wave, they slipped ahead tree by tree. Somewhere on the mountain behind them, a bitch wolf's sharp howl carried down the slope and raised the hair on the back of Slocum's neck. Her huskier mate's cry answered her, and when Slocum heard the bitch again, she had gone over the ridge away from them.

His Colt was in hand, held close to his face so that he smelled the aroma of spent powder and of the fresh oil on the metal. With his shoulder pressed against the pitchy bark of the pine tree, he caught his breath and waited for the others. They soon took places to his right and left, like hands on a silent clock.

He raised his gaze to the rim on the east. The gray black sky offered no seam above the mountaintops. Soon it would lighten and the raid would begin. Bollinsky's men impressed him. They must be handpicked. His own experience with Mexican soldiers during the Apache wars had not impressed him with their bravery or skills. These men were tough rangers. He felt certain they would fight hard too.

Slocum rested against the large tree. He felt like he had been there before. Was it during the campaign against the Chiricahuas? Then he heard a rooster try to crow. Dawn couldn't be far away. Birds knew better than he did when sunup was at hand. The coolness swept his face and he wondered about Maria. The thoughts of her supple flesh warmed him in the chill. A shiver ran up his spine. He would much rather be in her bed at the moment, sharing the muscular body under her smooth skin, than with these men waiting for the bloodshed that dawn would bring on.

8

"No quarter for the enemy," were Bollinsky's orders. Screams of the charging soldiers rushing the *rancheria* shattered the canyon's silence. The crack of rifle shots sounded off like Chinese firecrackers. From his position on the edge of the camp, Slocum watched the panic-driven outlaws rush out of their hovels into the face of death. Dogs howled in pain and fear. Some of the gang members made it through the first hail of bullets, and mounted horses bareback, only to be cut down by the deadly cross fire of the soldiers.

In a few minutes, only the sobbing of the camp women could be heard, and the moaning cries of the wounded. Without sympathy, the soldiers dragged the still-living outlaws to the corral and lashed them to the top rails so they were forced to stand side by side. Bloody, some unconscious, they hung like ravaged, bloody rag dolls.

Bollinsky stalked across the camp slapping his palm with his crop.

"Where is Lobo?" he demanded.

"Dead, I guess, Captain," his sergeant offered.

"No! Somehow he has escaped! Send some men for our horses and then shoot each one of these between the eyes." He pointed at the wounded ones.

"*Sí, capitán.*"

Slocum saw the rage written on the captain's face. How had the outlaw leader gotten away? With care, Slocum reloaded his Colt and considered the situation. His thoughts were shattered by the loud crack of pistol shots. The executions had begun.

Screams of camp women mixed with the individual pistol rounds as each outlaw was disposed of. Even the seeming dead were shot again in the head to take no chances. That job completed, Bollinsky's men began to drag the bereaved women away to the hovels. Obviously, to use their bodies for their own pleasure. To the victor went the spoils, and flesh looked like the best treasure his men could find in this place. Bollinsky ignored the actions of his men.

"Raphael has gone to search for his tracks," he announced to Slocum. "Lobo will not escape."

"But like a wolf away from his den, he'll be harder to trap now that he knows you are after him."

"Exactly." Bollinsky looked away at the high peaks. "Much harder, except he has no provisions."

"These people in the mountains will clothe and shelter him."

"Then they too will pay a harsh price for their efforts to aid him."

"You hardly need me for this search. I plan to return to the hacienda," Slocum said.

"I understand. You disapprove of my methods."

"No, you have a job to do."

"These killers did not give the don any quarter. They deserve none themselves."

Slocum nodded. Actually, he felt the man's actions were too severe, but he wasn't responsible for the safety of the law-abiding either. If the law across the border used the same tactics, criminals like Montrose might not be plaguing the land.

"I will miss your company," Bollinsky offered. "To have an intelligent person to talk to is rare for me."

"Perhaps our paths will cross again. Good luck in finding him. He needs removal."

"There are women here, if you wish one." Bollinsky swept his hand toward the hovels with some disdain.

"No, thanks."

"I agree. They are a slovenly lot. I see the private is bringing up our horses. Give my regards to the Señorita Obregon."

"I'll do that. Good luck in finding Lobo," Slocum said with a wave.

Mounted, he turned his back on the camp and set out over the ridge. He was a long ways from Maria's. There was little doubt in his mind that Bollinsky would find Lobo. The captain was thorough and definitive in his ways. Too much so at times to be comfortable company for Slocum.

In mid-afternoon, he made the twisting ride down to the canyon floor. Heat waves reflected off the rock walls, and the gorge became an oven. At last on the floor, he rested the bay and waited until he recovered. He wondered if Bollinsky had yet had any success in finding Lobo. Then he mounted up and headed west.

Under a spray of stars in the night, a guard challenged him at the perimeter of the hacienda.

"I'm Slocum."

"Sí, Señor."

"Is everything all right?"

"No signs of the outlaws since you left, Señor."

"Good. Take care, be on your guard. Lobo escaped the soldiers in the mountains."

"Bad news."

"Yes, but his gang is no more. They will get him too."

"Let us hope so."

Slocum rode between the fields and vineyards. He entered the walled yard after speaking to the guard there. It must be after midnight. He unsaddled at the barn area. Soon a young man came and sleepily apologized for not being there sooner to help him.

"No problem." Slocum glanced toward the house and seeing a light, decided someone was up. "Give him a generous helping of grain, he's been many miles," he told the stable boy.

At the boy's nod, Slocum headed for the house. His back felt stiff and his legs were like lead. A young woman opened the door at his knock, and gasped.

"Oh, Señor, you have returned."

"Is something wrong?"

"No, but Maria said to awaken her when you returned."

"Let her sleep."

"No, she would be too upset."

"Is there any food in the kitchen?" he asked, obviously unable to dissuade the girl from waking Maria.

"Yes, I will have Anita to fix some."

"Don't get the poor girl up too."

"No problem, Maria will want her to."

"Doesn't sound like I have any say."

"Oh, yes, Señor, but I must awaken her at once." The poor upset girl wrung her hands.

Slocum waved her away. Then he headed down the candlelit hall for the kitchen. There were times when he wanted things simpler than what was presented to him. Getting everyone up in the middle of the night was not his purpose. Besides, he was dog-tired, dirty, and stiff from the ride. He could hear the servant girl's shouting. He closed his eyes for a moment in the doorway to the great kitchen.

"Slocum! Slocum!" Maria cried out, and rushed into the room.

He rose from the great wooden chair and took her into

his arms. She kissed him and pressed her ripe body against him.

"I have been so worried."

"Nothing happened to me. Didn't even come close."

"Did you get him?"

"No." He shook his head wearily and they separated. "But they got all of his gang."

"How did he escape?" she asked, taken aback by the news.

"He's elusive. They'll get him."

"Montrose is in Nogales. One of my men brought us word yesterday and said that he is hiring men to raid the ranch." She frowned at him.

"He comes here, we will give him a welcome he won't forget."

Her shoulder trembled in an obvious shudder. "I'm afraid."

"Don't be. I am here now. Your men can handle them."

"But they are only *peones* against *pistoleros*. I mean, how can they?"

"Most of the men he will hire are riffraff, scum, and they have no stomach for opposition. They thrive on cowering over the unprotected, those who can't fight back. Resistance in any form will turn their stomachs and minds to retreating to where they are safe."

"I hope you are right. Anita is cooking you some food."

"Yes. I never intended to wake up the whole hacienda."

"Do you wish a bath?" she asked, ignoring his apology.

He nodded in defeat. "Yes, but—"

"Quit worrying so. Teeyah, go warm some bathwater for him," she told the girl who'd opened the front door earlier. The girl scurried off to obey.

"What will you do next?" Maria asked.

"Go to Nogales and learn what I can about Montrose's plans."

"Oh, that would be too dangerous." A concerned look swept her face in the candlelight.

"One way that we can be ready for him is know his intentions."

"But what if—"

He shook his head to dismiss her concerns. It was imperative to at least know the strength of the man's forces. How much border trash could Montrose hire anyway? He would speak to her man Franco in the morning about the hacienda's defenses.

The rich dishes of beans, goat cheese, and beefsteak filled his empty stomach and made him sleepy. Afterwards, he took a bath in a copper tub set up in her bedroom. She brought him a robe to wear. Then she disappeared with an armload of his clothing. Clean at last, he rose to his feet, and the water rushed from him in sheets. She hurried back in the room armed with a towel to dry him.

"I will worry about you going to Nogales," she said, on her knees, busy drying his legs and feet.

"I will be all right."

Then her fist enclosed his shaft and gently tugged on it. He glanced downward, realizing her intentions, but all he could see in the flickering light was the top of her head. His throat felt bottomless when her lips touched the sensitive head. Then her lips softly parted and he rose on his toes, filled with anticipation at his entry into her hot mouth. Her free hand clutched the back of his calves, her fingernails dug in his flesh. Then the flickering abrasion of her hot tongue on the underside of his glans sent bolts of lightning up his spine.

His fingers combed through her hair until they locked behind her ears, and he squeezed his eyes shut to hold off the forces of explosion. Her mouth pumped the shaft. He felt himself falling off a mountain, swept in an avalanche of fury. His sword became rock-hard in her fiery cavern, and the skin became painfully tight.

Then she began to cradle and fondle his scrotum. The ache in his gonads became excruciating from the manipulation of her gentle massage. He drove his hips forward with a strain that cramped both balls, and felt the explosion leave the base of his cannon. It shot out of the muzzle in a sharp flare of pain that made him wonder if the burning head of his dick wasn't split apart.

In dreamy wonder, he pulled her to her feet and began to kiss her with a fury. She moaned and threw her arms around him. With the salty taste of his semen on her lips, her fiery mouth pressed to his like a great suction force. They whirled off into another world. He swept her into his arms and carried her to the great feather bed.

In seconds, she was undressed, her blouse pushed up high enough for him to taste her rock-hard nipples and feast on them. Between her silky legs he felt the return of his erection. Soon her fingers began to play with him, and he sucked harder on her breast.

Anxious for his entry, she pulled hard on his shaft. When he was only half hard, she impatiently slipped him in her lubricated gates. She threw her head back and cried out loud, "Yes!"

He felt himself quickly balloon. The tender surface of the glans was so sore, each stroke proved painful. But another force drove him on, despite the discomfort; a basic gut-driven need made him harder and harder.

She threw her head back on the pillow and cried out in unrestrained pleasure. Her legs kicked high above his back, and she squirmed to lift her hips up until their pubic bones rubbed their coarse body hair together. He wondered if the servants could hear her moans and screams.

Then she issued a sharp gasp, and with a flood of hot fluids from her vagina, she collapsed. He could see in the faint light her dazzled eyes. The smile creased her full lips and she moaned, "Slocum, don't ever leave me."

He kissed her softly. Then he closed his eyes to the bitterness of his own reality. *God, girl, you will never know how much I wish I could stay forever.*

9

The guitar and trumpet music from the cantinas floated on the night's soft breeze. A faint aroma of bougainvillea flowers, mingled with the sour smell of liquor, cheap *puta* perfume, and the stink of horse piss, filled his nose. Hitched at racks, horses filled the narrow hilly street, half asleep and standing hip-shot before the whorehouses and saloons where their riders had gone inside for business or sport. Nogales, Sonora, was a man's town filled with the pleasures of drink and flesh for the freighters, cowboys, and miners from the nearby mines.

A place where many wanted men stayed, barely beyond the grasp of American law, still close enough to their homeland not to forget their citizenship. The kind of men who would sell their grandmothers into white slavery for a small price. In rooms clouded with smoke, smugglers sat around tables under wavering candlelight and schemed how to get contraband into the U.S. and not pay the tariff on it.

With his own purpose in mind, Slocum ambled his way down the flat stone sidewalk, past the lighted doorways of the cantinas. He escaped the grasp of enterprising *putas*, who stood out front of their establishments in search of customers and reached with brazen familiarity for his crotch. With a shake of his head and gently waving their arms aside, he strode on, making certain no one else noticed his passing.

"May your donkey dick be stricken with clap and never get hard again!" one of the doves shouted in defiance after him.

He grinned at her angry tirade of words at his back. Then he slipped into the dark alleyway and waited a few minutes. If anyone had followed him, they would soon show themselves. No one came by except some drunk *vaqueros,* who staggered past from the opposite direction and never spotted him in the shadowy confines. They were too inebriated and busy bragging about their latest conquest to notice a thing. *Why, I screwed her so hard, she finally cried in pain that my hard-on was too big and why did I last forever.*

When the one of them said, "Yeah, and your two minutes was up," Slocum shook his head in amusement.

With a quick check of the street, he crossed it, then slipped into the opposite alley, found a flight of stairs, and went up to the second floor. He could see over the flat roofs while he waited for someone to answer his knock.

"Go away," a small voice said. "She is getting ready for work."

"Tell her Slocum is here," he said under his breath. He stared at the peeling paint on the door's panels in the starlight, impatient for this person to open it.

"I must ask her first."

"Fine, I'll be here." He scanned the crowded cluster of building roofs on the hillside and waited. Below in a courtyard, Chinese lanterns lighted some couples dancing. A trumpet shattered the night, and the click of castanets kept time. The shrill laughter of whores and their half-drunk lovers' whoops carried on the soft wind.

The door creaked open an inch. Then, as if satisfied,

the small figure in a white nightgown opened it for him to enter. "Come in, Señor."

"*Gracias.*" He took off his hat and nodded.

"Follow me." A girl in her teens in a housecoat led the way through the narrow dark hallway with only one candle to light the way.

She opened a door and stepped back. The room's light was too brilliant for an instant until his eyes adjusted. Dressed in a pink girdle that hugged her round form and seated at the dressing table, Millie Monroe swiveled her chubby short legs around on the bench to appraise him.

"Sweet Jesus, what brings you here?"

"I need some information."

"Ha." She made a peeved face at him. "I knew it wasn't my sensuous body you came after."

"Not this time."

"Good. I'd want to get all heated up a few days in preparation before you came. So be sure to send word so I can plan to be ready for you." She turned back to the mirror and applied powder to her face.

"Business must be good," he said, looking around the room at the fine furniture.

"I deal cards. And do well. Men like to look at my tits and imagine what they would look like out of this damn corset. Gives me an edge. But what do you want?" Then she made a displeased face at him when he did not instantly answer her. "They sag some now. So what?"

"I'd bet they're as pretty as ever," he said, and grinned at her.

"Slocum, you could smooth-talk a bitch alligator out of a lay."

"I'm not here for that, Millie. I need to know about an American. His name is Montrose. An outlaw. He's gathering men here to raid a friend's hacienda."

"Montrose, huh?" She squeezed her cleft chin. There was something about Millie—the seductive flair of her

short fingers and the way she moved her hands around
her bare creamy neck, exposed cleavage, and smooth
shoulders. The extra flesh she'd gained did not distract
from her either, only made a man's groin stir even more
in her presence.

"I have to go deal cards in twenty minutes. Make yourself at home until I get back. I'll find out what I can about
him for you. Those brothers still after you?"

"Abbott brothers? Yes."

"Damn shame, or we could go to Alaska together and
get ass-rich up there. That don't count the benefits of you
and me sleeping together in a ship's cabin all the way up
there." She nodded her head as if she knew the answer to
her proposition without his reply. "I'll find out about this
Montrose. Hold your horses. Stay here. You can wait a
few hours for a good thing." Then she smiled seductively
at him. "I'll have my girl Imogene fix you some supper.
You look to me like you missed a few meals."

She raised the frilly green silk dress over her head, and
ducked under it to emerge switching the waist around to
suit her. She glanced at the smoky mirror before the dressing table, then took a brush to her long curly brown hair.

"I never dreamed you'd come see me again." She stood
up, holding the dress with her elbows against her body,
and backed towards him. "Button me up."

"I never left mad." He closed up the dress. Her sweet
perfume wafted up his nose and tickled the senses in his
brain.

"No, I remember when you left me. Those damn Abbott
brothers were downstairs." She shook her head in disapproval. "Think about going to Alaska with me while I'm
gone." She kissed him on the cheek and left the room.
Then she stuck her head back in. "Supper is coming and
don't screw my help."

He waved her away and went to the door that led onto
the rooftop. Outside in the cool night breeze, he drew a

cigar from his pocket, struck a lucifer on a post, and took a seat in the hammock. A few hours' wait for the information he needed didn't bother him. The sweetness of the smoke filled his mouth and he exhaled. His hat set aside, he stretched out on the hammock and savored the cigar. If anyone in Nogales could learn what he needed to know about Montrose, Millie could. He studied the star-pricked sky and the red glow of his stub each time he drew in on it. What in the hell would he do in Alaska?

The girl brought him some enchiladas and tortillas on a tray. He sat up and thanked her.

"You need a light to see by?" she asked.

"No," he said. "I can see fine."

"I'm going to get you a bottle of wine. Is red okay?"

"It'll be fine."

"She doesn't have any whiskey."

"Who drank it?" he asked softly, glancing up at her.

"Don Montoya."

"Is he very rich?"

"I think so. He is about the only one she lets come up here. I was surprised she let you in."

He nodded, and held the wad of a tortilla ready to put in his mouth. "We go way back. Why are you here?"

"I must get the wine." She turned and ran for the door.

He guessed her to be American—she spoke good English. No telling where Millie had found her. Millie gathered strays the way some people picked up all the abandoned dogs.

"You need a glass?" the girl asked, returning with his wine.

"No. What's your name? She told me, but I have forgotten."

"Imogene."

"How did you get here?" He took the bottle and pointed the neck toward a chair for her to sit in.

"Millie bought me from a Chinaman."

"How did he get you?" A wave of revulsion made him shake his head. The notion that a young girl like her had been in the hands of some whoremonger made him half sick.

"I ran away."

"From home?" he asked between bites. For a long moment, he tried to see her face, but it was too dark to make out much more than the oval outline.

"Yes. My father made me sleep with him," she said quickly.

"I see."

"My mother took alkali poisoning on some bad water that we drank coming out here from Texas. She got real puny. Out of her head for days, and when he'd try to get in bed with her, she would scream and have a fit. He said to me that he needed a woman real bad and I wasn't supposed to say nothing to her or my younger sister Lacey about what we did. Told me, as the oldest, it was my duty to do that for him."

"It was hard for you to do it, wasn't it?" He glanced up to see her bob her head in agreement.

"Made me sick, and besides, he hurt me. You know. I thought once would be enough, but it wasn't. He got so he became obsessed to do it all the time, even in the broad daylight. He'd stop the wagon in the middle of the day. Send Lacey off on some dumb errand, make me bend over and raise up my skirts, so he could poke it in me."

"Your maw ever figure it out?"

"She did, but she was bedfast and could only cry about it. One time when he wasn't looking, she give me three dollars and said when I found a chance to run off, for me to run away from him. That he was mad, crazy."

"How did you get away?"

"We was camped at Shakespeare on the New Mexico border. Needed a rim welded on one of our wagon wheels. A Chinese man came by selling wares out of a wagon. I told him that night if he would take me to Tucson, I'd pay him three dollars."

"Did he take you to Tucson?" Slocum looked up at her. She shook her head. He understood, and swiped the plate clean with the last tortilla. "What happened then?"

"I soon found I had traded one rutting boar for another."

"Bad, huh?"

"Yes. He told me I could either let him use my body or he would sell me to the Apaches."

"Did he know any?"

"Yes. He traded with some the first day we left Shakespeare on the road to Mexico. They were filthy and smelled bad. I felt certain he would do that, so I became his mistress."

"He sold you to Millie? This Chinaman?"

"After a month." She shook her head, crossed her legs, and jerked the hem of her shift down defensively. "Actually, he lost me in a card game to her. She's been very kind to me."

"A good gal," he said.

"How do you know her?"

"Oh, we met in Dodge a few years back. In my cattle-driving days. Then I learned she was here and looked her up a few years ago. Some bounty hunters interrupted my stay here the last time."

"You're wanted?" she asked breathlessly.

"By some. What's your family name?"

"Teller. Why?"

"Just curious. That's your father's name."

"Norrel Teller is his name."

Slocum nodded, and swigged the wine from the neck of the bottle. It was good enough, not too sweet. His meal finished, he felt relaxed for the first time in weeks. He wouldn't soon forget the old man's name. Maybe someday their paths would cross and he could even the score for Imogene. What went around came around in this old world.

She rose and looked off across the roofs with her back to him. The gentle night wind stirred the thin shift she wore, and the starlight illuminated the white material and showed her slender figure through it.

"Will my life ever be normal again?" she asked.

"What do you want to be?"

"Be someone's wife, have children. Will I marry a man like my father and not know it?" She glanced back at him for a reply.

"Lots of questions. Yes, Imogene, you will find a man, have children of your own, and chances are good that he won't ever do to his daughters what happened to you."

"You sound so certain. I keep thinking I belong down there." She bowed her head towards the laughter and noise coming from below them.

"That's up to you. But it's a short life down there. Only a few ever manage to do what Millie is doing."

"I used to dream that a man would ride up and take me for his bride."

"Keep watching for him."

She gave a loud sigh, then turned. "Did you get enough to eat?"

"Plenty. Thanks."

"I better go to bed. Good night, Slocum," she said, and went to the doorway.

"Good night, Imogene."

He sat on the edge of the hammock and savored the rest of the wine. Imogene was a tender child ripped into bitter reality by the actions of a boar hog. Plenty of bad men on the frontier, outlaws and incestuous fathers and fornicators, besides El Lobo and Montrose. After hearing her story, he could add Norrel Teller's name to his list of worthless no-accounts in the West.

•   •   •

"Wake up and move over."

Slocum opened his left eye, and could see Millie in a frilly silk gown standing there at the edge of the hammock in the starlight. He grinned at her, then with some effort made room for her on the springy bed.

"You didn't think my information came free, did you?" she asked.

"No, ma'am."

"Then get your pants off. Hell, you're fully dressed."

He rolled off the hammock, stood up, and undressed. The cool night air moved over his bare skin when he climbed back in.

"What did you learn?" he asked.

"This Montrose is staying at a small ranch south of here." She tugged on her gown and scooted closer to him.

"What else?"

"He's hiring *pistoleros*." With her right hand, she swept the curls back from her face.

"How many does he have hired?" He slipped his arm under her head and eased himself closer to her.

"Not enough." She snuggled until their bellies met.

"Not enough?"

Then she laid a finger on his lips. "I sent a spy to learn all about it. We will soon hear from him. Now . . ." She raised herself up and swept the gown under her so that her legs and butt were bare. "You get on top. You know, doing this with you was all I could think about while dealing cards tonight."

He rose on the swinging hammock and suppressed his amusement when they swung perilously from side to side. At last situated between her snowy legs on the gentle waving bed, he felt her small fingers begin to pull on his shaft with impatience.

He bent over and kissed her puffy lips. Then he arched his back under her direction until she poked him inside her slick velvet gates. With the rippling movement of the hammock, he began to explore the depths of her hot sheath. She issued soft moans, and hunched herself to help him go deeper. Her short legs soon wrapped around his back, and the muscles inside her began to contract on his swelling manhood with each thrust.

Their back-and-forth motion became greater, and the hammock's actions made it even more exaggerated. His hips ached for more and more of her. Soon they were being tossed like a small ship at sea, until at last she cried out loud, threw her head back, and strained.

He felt the volley of cannon fire rush from the depths of his scrotum. It painfully exploded from the head as if the bore was too small for its escape, and they collapsed in a fluid-filled connection of exhaustion.

A cool wind swept over his perspiration-dampened skin. Thoughts about Montrose's plans circulated in his mind. Then they fell asleep in each other's arms.

Late the next afternoon, Pasco came to her place. He was a small, unassuming man in the white cotton clothing of a *peon* and with a great palm-frond hat with a Chihuahua crown. He stood with it in his hands. She waved him over to sit in a chair, and asked what he had learned.

"This man Montrose has maybe ten men hired, but he wants thirty."

"Are they tough men?" she asked, then looked over at Slocum, who had said nothing.

"No. They are cowards. But enough cowards makes an army, no?"

Slocum nodded from where he sat in the wicker chair. Enough of them, well-armed, made a force to be reckoned with. And greater numbers would make them even more dangerous.

"What is he doing about it?" Slocum asked. "To get more men."

"He said he would pay me twenty pesos for every man I could find to ride with him."

"Wow, he is desperate," she said.

Slocum agreed with her assessment, and turned back to Pasco. "Who is there at this ranch besides Montrose?"

"Two gringos—they are young and twirl their pistols all the time." Pasco made a face that he was not impressed.

"Yes, I know them. One is Hobby, the blonde, and the other is Bow. Was there an older man, a gringo?"

"I never saw him."

"Who is he?" Millie asked.

"Montrose's other henchman, Wilton. He is the most dangerous one and stands back. If he wasn't there, he may be here in Nogales."

"What does that mean?" she asked with a peevish frown.

"He's cagey. Need to watch for him."

"How will you handle so many?" she asked with a concerned frown.

"Pick them off, a few a time."

She shook her head in disbelief. "You are loco." Displeasure written on her face, she turned to speak to Pasco. "If you hear anything else, let me know."

"I will, Señorita."

She went across the room for her purse, returned, and paid him in gold coins. Then she showed him to the door. Slocum sat back in the chair and wondered about the setup and what he could do.

"I'll repay you," he said, still deeply engrossed in his thoughts on how to stop the outlaws.

"You owe me nothing. Come, Imogene has food ready." She pulled him from the chair and slipped familiarly under his arm. "I would pay you to stay here with me."

"What would I do when that Don Montoya comes to see you?" he whispered.

"Just be discreet," she said with a disapproving look up at him.

"Oh, Millie, you are a wonder." He lowered his hand and playfully squeezed her hard butt.

She reached behind and captured his fingers. "My, my, and I have to soon go and deal cards. What will you do while I work?"

"Go look for Wilton. He's here somewhere if he's not at that ranch."

"Be careful," she said, taking a chair at the table. "My, Imogene, the food looks so good. She's a wonderful cook, isn't she?"

Slocum agreed, smiled across at the girl in approval, and sat down. He wondered where he would find Montrose's henchman. Wilton was there—all he had to do was find him. Come dark, he would locate the man.

10

Slocum checked several smoke-filled bar rooms, and
shared some whiskey with several scantily clad girls in
the cantinas. But none of the women recalled seeing the
older man he described. The night had grown late when
he entered the White Dove on the top of the Canal Street
Hill. Grateful for the thick fog of cigarette and cigar
smoke, he eased inside and moved along the wall, checking faces and outlines. If Wilton wore the same felt Stetson, Slocum would recognize the dip in the brim. Hats
became a man's trademark after he wore them any time
at all.

He spotted the back of Wilton's hat, and took an empty
chair at a distance from where the man sat. With his own
Stetson pulled down, and leaning forward with his elbows
on the table, Slocum tried to observe what the man was
doing.

A *puta* sat down in the chair beside the man. He must
be buying her "tea." It was what they served the bar girls,
but the man paid the price for bottle-and-bond whiskey.

Slocum could hear the chorus of the girls. "You buy
me whiskey, mister?" He wondered how long he dared
stay there. If Wilton was inebriated enough, he might

never notice him. Then three drunks came over from the bar and stood before the outlaw.

"You need *pistoleros*, hombre?" the one in the middle asked, wavering until he leaned forward and his hands grasped the back of the chair.

"You three *pistoleros*?" Wilton asked in a coarse voice.

"Damn right and plenty bad hombres," the man said.

"Sit down, boys," Wilton said. "I need plenty bad hombres."

Slocum noticed that several whores immediately rushed over to the table like chickens to a grain scattering. Soon each man had a willing dove on his lap, and Wilton poured the round of drinks for his newly hired employees. Obviously, Wilton intended to give them enough booze and pleasures so they did not have second thoughts about not becoming *pistoleros*. They called it "shanghaiing" in Frisco. When ships were short crew members, unscrupulous recruiters gave the sailors-to-be a grand night of free liquor and pussy. However, to their disappointment, the partygoers awoke the next day with splitting headaches at sea.

Slocum had seen enough. Shaking his head at the barmaid, who at last came to take his order, he left the White Dove. It would be several hours before Wilton left the party. Perhaps Slocum could go back to Millie's and nap until then. Somehow he needed to stop this recruitment process. If Montrose had no men to ride with him, then he wouldn't dare try to raid the hacienda. Time would be short. Slocum searched his mind for a way to upset their plans.

He needed to find Pasco. It would be daylight before he could do that. There might be one way to stop Montrose before his gang grew into an army.

At dawn, Slocum, wearing a serape and straw hat for a disguise, stood back and watched the hungover men stumble out of the back door of the whorehouse. Armed with bottles of tequila and mescal, they climbed into the wooden-wheeled *carteria* with some effort, and after taking their seats for the ride, they covered themselves with their serapes against the cool air.

They cheered and waved back at the line of whores crowded in the doorway to see them off. Soon Wilton came out and nodded for the old driver to take them away. Then he turned and counted out money to the big Mexican who obviously owned the place.

The ungreased cart axle whined in protest when the sleepy steers began to pull it. The clatter of the wooden wheels on the cobblestone street joined in, and somewhere a rooster crowed. More *pistoleros* were headed for Montrose's army. Slocum wondered where Wilton would go next. Obviously he was busy talking with the owner about their recruiting success and how to get more men that night.

Slocum eased back in the doorway and waited. Wilton soon went by and down the winding hill street. With a push away from the door, Slocum took up pursuit. He wanted to learn more about the man's daytime activities. Whenever he caught sight of the man's heels, he slipped back in a doorway or between a building and let him continue on.

At last, he saw Wilton disappear in a building marked Grande Hotel, a two-story adobe structure with window boxes festooned with flowers. Perhaps Pasco could ferret out more about the man. Slocum turned on his heel and went back to Millie's.

Pasco came quickly when Millie sent Imogene with the note that she needed to see him. He joined Slocum and Millie for their mid-morning meal of oranges, melons, grapes, and other fruit. Millie, in her flowery silk dressing gown, rose and waved the man over to a chair.

"I found Wilton last night in the White Dove," Slocum said. "He recruited six men with mescal and women."

"I have heard of this man since we talked last," said Pasco.

"Eat something," Millie said, indicating Pasco should help himself to the spread of fruits on the table.

"I have eaten breakfast, *gracias*." He turned to Slocum. "A man named Rosallis owns that place."

"Big man. I saw Wilton pay him this morning." Slocum peeled a red Mexican banana to eat. "Wilton is staying at the Grande Hotel. I followed him there."

Pasco nodded.

"I want you to find some cheap whores. I don't care if they have crabs and the clap," Slocum said to the man. "And some cheap rum—we will need barrels of it."

Millie made a face of disapproval at his words, then went on feeding herself whole red grapes.

"What do you wish for me to do then?" Pasco asked.

"There aren't any women at this ranch of Montrose's, is there?"

"No." Pasco shrugged. "Maybe one or two old women who cook."

"Good. Then I want the cheapest whores that you can hire and some cheap liquor. Lots of it for him and his army out there."

"How will we do it?"

"You find them and pay someone with carts to take them out there. The women better arrive about dark, so Montrose won't suspect too much. Tell them they get two pesos for each man they lay. And give each one of the women a double eagle for going beforehand."

"Ten dollars would be enough. Too much money might start talk and clean ones would want to go." Pasco sat back in the chair and grinned at Slocum's plan. "It is a very mean trick."

"Hungover and worn out, they won't want to fight much, will they?"

"Oh, no."

"Later, I want to look over this place of his. How do I get there?"

Pasco gave him the details of the route. Slocum paid the man enough to hire the girls and buy two kegs of cheap rum. Then the man excused himself and went off to recruit some of the low-life women from the street and a driver to get them and the liquor up there.

"I suppose you are going to ride out there?" Millie asked Slocum.

"I better. Need a feel for all this business."

"How did you ever think of this plan to stop him?"

"Just came to me early this morning watching all of them come out of that whorehouse. Besides, a stiff dick has no conscience."

"Oh, I agree with that. You be careful riding out there. This Montrose sounds like a mean one."

"He is. One of the toughest I ever met. He's like a bulldog all the time."

"What's he going to do when he discovers you fixed all his *pistoleros*?"

"What can he do?"

"Be pissed off, I guess." She pulled apart the peeled orange in her hands and slipped a segment into her mouth.

"He needs that too."

She waved a short finger at him, swallowed hard, and managed to say, "You be careful today."

"I will," he said. He leaned over, kissed her lightly on the mouth, and standing up, put on his straw sombrero.

It was mid-afternoon when he looked over the ranch. He took care to ride around it so his brass telescope lens would not reflect the sun. In the eyepiece, he could make out a few adobe buildings and some stick corrals. A fresh stack of hay for the riding stock stood nearby. It had obviously been hauled into this place, for there was little graze around the buildings. Goats darted about the camp and bleated. Several of the men took siestas on their bed-rolls under some palm-frond ramadas.

He spotted the blond head of Hobby among the sleepers. By Slocum's count there were close to twenty men in the shade. All he needed to do was wait for Pasco's "girls" to arrive in a few hours, and the party would begin.

He eased back. There was no sign of Montrose, but his black, half-Percheron horse was in the corrals. He had seen the proud arched neck and split mane of the big animal. The man must be inside one of the buildings taking a nap. He might be wanted in Mexico too, and didn't dare show his face in public places like Nogales.

Satisfied, Slocum slipped back and collapsed the scope. He went and found his horse in the draw, and took a swig from the canteen on the saddlehorn. He spent the afternoon in the wash, out of sight, listening and whittling on sticks.

Late evening, he took up his position again. He could smell the mesquite smoke fires, and watched the two older women serving a meal to the gang. Then from the north came the creak of an ox cart. Several of the men with their plates in hand looked in that direction.

He saw Montrose, with the sombrero on his shoulders, lean against the corner of a building, observing all that happened. Obviously, the outlaw was wondering about a cart coming uninvited to his hideout at this time of day.

Soon the cheering and shouting of the women in the conveyance sent men running to see them. Pasco had done well. There were a half-dozen women, whom the men graciously helped down. Someone found a guitar and a fiddle, and the fiesta began.

Slocum watched the big man questioning one of the women. He heard her very loudly shout, "Wilton sent us!"

A smile on his mouth, Slocum edged backwards. He needed to ride to the hacienda and get him some men. If his plan worked, after daybreak they could take the camp and the stricken *pistoleros* would be no problem to disarm.

In the wash, he tightened the cinch on the bay and then swung up in the saddle. With the north star to his left, he headed for Maria's.

Hours later, a sleepy-sounding guard challenged him at the edge of the vineyards.

"Slocum here."

"Ah, *sí, Señor.* Good to see you again."

"All well at the ranch?"

"No problems."

"Good, keep an eye out. Lobo is still loose, remember."

"Oh, *sí, Señor.*"

Slocum jogged the bay down the dusty road between the staked vines that spilled profusely. Their large leaves reflected the moonlight, and deep underneath, he knew the green fruit had already begun to swell up like a pregnant woman's belly. He hoped someday Maria found the right man to help her oversee this place. So many families in Mexico depended on the hacienda system for their livelihood. Most residents on such holdings lived much better lives than the independents who, without capital or a way to raise it, could hardly grow enough corn for their own family to exist on.

The guard over the gate, armed with a rifle, nodded his approval, and Slocum rode around the wagons set up to block the gate from an attack. Good, they were still on guard. He had worried they might have become complacent in his absence. Until they eliminated both Lobo and Montrose, they needed tight security.

A boy rushed into the moonlight to take his horse when he dismounted. Slocum nodded and clapped him on the shoulder for being so intent on doing his job. He crossed the dark shadowy courtyard and entered through the kitchen, hoping not to wake anyone. He planned to find the largest chair in the great dining hall and sleep in it until sunup.

His boot soles sounded gritty on the tile, but he managed to slip through the kitchen with only one flickering candle in the holder to show the way. At last he felt the night winds flowing through the dark dining area. His gunbelt undone, he eased himself down in a chair and set the holster on the floor with his hat. He sat back to nap for a little while before he would send word to Franco to get ready to ride.

The burst of cannonballs deafened him. He rode a sorrel horse in a hard run, and the incoming rounds exploded around his flight. His mount shied from the closer ones, but he reined him back on course. Corpses of men in gray uniforms dotted the grassy ground. His command waited in reserve on the left flank. He returned with orders to take them around behind the Yankee artillery and overrun the guns. It was a long shot, but if it worked, the chances of the Confederate forces taking the hill would be good.

Slocum lashed the red horse on despite the whistle in the animal's breathing. The horse was expendable. Despite his nagging conscience over the abuse, he had one obligation, to get behind the cannons and fast.

"Sergeant, mount up on the double!" he shouted, sawing the lathered horse to a halt.

In the confusion, his troops did well. Slocum took the lead on his hard-breathing charger, and started up the narrow farm road to the north. They should be out of the advance scouts' view. Slocum had the sergeant send out skirmishers, and they hit a lope. Time was precious.

Then a minié ball from a sniper's rifle sent the sorrel to his knees. Dismounted, revolver in his fist, Slocum looked about for the shooter. He ordered three men forward to find the shooter. A private brought him his own horse to ride.

Were the Yankees on to his scheme? Time clicked on, and their only chance was to overrun the artillery before troops were set up behind them. Scouts said the main force was three hours away—a crucial window that they needed to take advantage of, or more of his own would be slaughtered.

No time to check on whether there were reinforcements. When his men drew up to the left of the hill, he gave the order to charge and take the big guns at any cost. His troops rushed out of the woods like Indians on the war path. The small force of artillery men soon fell to his company's arms, many surrendering.

"Turn those guns around!" he screamed at his men.

In what seemed to him like hours, the artillery at last was reloaded and the rounds began to whistle off to the north. No matter about the target—the firepower counted.

Slocum glanced back, and could see men in ragtag uniforms and armed with rifles begin to race over the field of their own dead. Their Confederate cheers and shouts filled the air. Soon the ridge swarmed with friendly forces. Southern artillery pieces came on the fly to supplement the captured ones.

"You took what?" Maria asked, shaking him awake.

"Oh, a ridge that we needed," he managed, and scooted up. She stood wrapped in a white robe before him.

"Your back must be broken. Why did you not come to my bed?" she asked with a frown of disapproval.

"Didn't want to disturb you."

"I like to be disturbed—by you."

"I think I have Montrose stalled."

"Stalled?"

"I have a plan to cripple his army. It may work. I'll know soon enough."

"What else?"

"No word of El Lobo?" he asked.

"The rumors say he is still in the mountains."

"Good place for him."

"Are you hungry?"

"Always."

"Good," she said, looking a little peeved, and started for the kitchen.

He picked up his holster, slung it over his arm, and put on the straw hat. Food sounded wonderful. He recalled eating a red banana last. Then he headed after her for the kitchen.

He hung the gun and hat on a peg, and took her in his arms when she came back to him.

"I have been so worried," she said, fidgeting with the serape and not looking up. "You said you would leave me."

"Not yet. Good morning," he said to the two women who came in the room, so she would know they were not alone.

"Fix Slocum some food. He has not eaten in days," she said to the pair, and led him out of the room. After a check of the help's whereabouts, she pushed him against the wall with both hands and stood on her toes to kiss him.

"Gods, you worry me," she said at last.

"No need," he said with a smile for her. "We've been through lots rougher deals than this."

She looked to the ceiling for help. He swatted her teasingly on the butt. Lots worse than this.

11

Bollinsky and his company of *rurales* arrived before they finished breakfast. The officer strode into the house when the girl opened the door for him. He looked startled to see Slocum sitting there. The officer quickly recovered, but not before Slocum noticed the surprise in the man's face. At last, seated across from Slocum, the captain looked after Maria when she went to get more food arranged for.

"Lobo is gathering a new gang," Bollinsky said to Slocum, "according to what I can learn. He had some *indios*, some Yaquis and others, in his gang now."

"What's he doing for horses?"

"The mountain people must be furnishing them to him. We took or destroyed all the herd at the *rancheria*."

"I told you he had the allegiance of those people."

"He spends money with them, is what you mean?"

"Yes, that too."

"I want that man in my custody," Bollinsky said.

"I will help you if you will first arrest an outlaw called Montrose. He poses a greater threat to Maria than El Lobo does right now." Slocum felt better taking soldiers there rather than the hacienda people. Things had worked out well with Bollinsky's convenient arrival.

"Montrose Dulcia? He is here in Sonora?" Bollinsky frowned in disbelief at him.

"Planning a raid on this ranch too."

"I had no word he was here."

"Gathering up men. I was at his place last night."

"We ride at once."

"Good, they will be ready for you . . . " He let it trail off when she returned to the great room from the kitchen.

"Breakfast will be served in thirty minutes. Excuse me, I will get dressed," she said.

Both men rose for her, and she swished away.

"Your plan?" Bollinsky asked.

Slocum told him of the women and the mescal sent to the camp. Bollinsky nodded thoughtfully, then grinned. "Devilish idea."

"We sweep in there later today and they will be hungover and worn out. How much could they fight?"

"Grand idea. This Dulcia has many crimes to answer for."

"I thought so." Slocum stretched his arms over his head and flexed his sore back muscles. Things were going his way. He drew out a cigar, offered one to Bollinsky, who declined, and then struck a match to light it. Maybe too good.

Slocum, Bollinsky, and his soldiers were dismounted and rested in a dry wash near noon. The desert air carried the smell of creosote. Each man was ready to mount up, sweep in, and nip off Montrose's plans to raid Maria's hacienda.

They rose in the stirrups and quietly began to separate to approach the *rancheria*. In a line, they spread out in the desert greasewood, cactus, and scrub brush. Each man armed with a revolver in his fist, they made a formidable front advancing on the outlaws' lair as the sun's orb rose high in the sky.

"Gawdamn, the army's here!" A shocked man swore aloud, standing with his manhood in his hand, obviously unable to piss. When he raised his hands in the air, his exposed condition drew a grin from the soldier beside Slocum.

Others struggled from the bedrolls under the ramadas and raised their hands as the word spread. They were under siege by thirty armed and mounted *rurales* moving through their camp.

Then, from the front door of the hovel, Montrose rushed out with a Colt in each hand. He looked about for a second, then realizing their numbers, dropped the revolvers in defeat.

"Montrose Dulcia, you're under arrest," Bollinsky announced.

"Son of a bitch, it's you, Slocum." The big man ignored the captain while two soldiers handcuffed his hands and legs.

"Yeah, sure hate this too." Slocum suppressed his amusement. He turned around and saw they had Hobby and Bow arrested too. All they needed was Wilton. Then the entire gang could rot in a Mexican federal prison for the rest of time.

"Don't touch the women," Bollinsky's sergeant reminded his men. "They may all have crabs and the clap."

"How the hell do you know that?" Montrose demanded as they shoved him toward the others.

"I sent them to you," Slocum said, and laughed aloud.

"Then damn ugly whores that came up here last night?" Montrose paused despite the efforts of his captors to shove him on toward the others.

"That was them."

"They said Wilton sent them." Montrose's thick eyebrows formed a hard line as he stared up at him.

"You ever know a whore to tell the truth?"

Montrose jerked away again. "I'll get your ass, Slocum. You wait and see. I'll get you."

"My, my, for a man facing life in prison, you sound quite tough," Bollinsky said, amused.

"You too—" A soldier's rifle butt struck hard to his back silenced the outlaw leader's threat, and he staggered forward.

"I will take these men to the prison. And meet you at the hacienda in a week," Bollinsky said to Slocum. "Then we can go after Lobo."

Slocum agreed, seeing that all the would-be outlaws were under control. That the gang was captured made him feel better. His plan had worked.

"What about Wilton?" he asked Bollinsky, reminded that the number-two man was still free.

"The Nogales police will arrest him before he has word of this. I've sent a man to inform them to hold him for me."

"You're taking all of these to the state prison?"

"Of course. They will have their trial there."

"Didn't worry me. They can't buy their way out of there, can they?"

"No. Why do you ask?"

"I figure that Wilton can buy his way out of that local calaboose in Nogales before the sun sets."

Bollinsky nodded grimly. "I will send Corporal Anton and two men to bring him here then."

"Good idea." Slocum felt better about the entire matter. That way Montrose's entire gang would be in jail. Less chance for them to get away from the flimsy, corrupt local penal system where a peso was stronger than a judge's orders.

He adjusted his cinch and remounted. "I'll go back and make sure nothing happens at the hacienda. Have a safe journey."

"Thanks again," Bollinsky said, and nodded toward the

blond-headed Bow, frantically scratching his privates like a man possessed. "He caught them from those cheap *putas* you sent them."

"Better treat your men for the buggers after you leave this bunch off at jail." Slocum swung up and rose in the stirrup to ride off.

"Gawdamn you, Slocum!" Montrose swore after him. "I'll nail your ass to a damn cross!"

Slocum disregarded the threat, and felt better than he had in weeks. He short-loped the bay toward the hacienda. On the ridge he looked back. The *rurales* had their prisoners seated on the ground. Another chapter in his life was shut down. Good enough. He was anxious to get on with something else besides looking over his shoulder expecting to see Montrose's ugly face.

He reached the hacienda in mid-afternoon. He passed men busy irrigating the chest-high cornfields from small ditches. They looked up and waved at his passage. Others hoed in the fields of beans and melons, and acknowledged him.

Maria ran from the house and hugged him.

"You are safe. Oh, thank God." She rested her head on his chest.

"Montrose and his men are prison-bound."

"No one was shot or killed?"

"No."

"How did you take him that way?"

"Outnumbered and surrounded him."

"Can you stay longer?"

"I promised Bollinsky I would stay over and help him track down El Lobo."

"When will he come for you?"

"In a week."

She made a face, and then shook her head in surrender. "Franco wants to take those cattle to market."

"I'll stay here and watch things until he returns."

"Good." She wrapped his arm over her shoulder and led him to the house. "And tonight, you will sleep with me."

"As you say," he said softly.

12

He awoke in the night. She breathed softly on her side, and he eased himself off the bed. His plans were to let her sleep. The soft wind swept the curtains from the bedroom windows. He stood at the sill and stared into the starlighted courtyard. Her hacienda was such a paradise to live on, and the two of them were so well suited for one another. They made such passionate lovers. He closed his eyes to the thought of when he must part with her. Then, in the distance, he saw a match flare.

A brief burst of yellow, and then the light was gone. Was Lobo out there? He found his holster and hat. With his boots in his hand to quietly make his exit, he hurried down the halls. He put on his boots seated on the front porch. Who was out there beyond the fields? A spy or a gang? Must be long past midnight. Hardly a chance it was one of the hacienda people. The guards had strict orders never to light a match.

Quietly, he took a horse from the stables, saddled him, and left the building. He waved to the guard over the gate, and the man nodded at him. When he rode underneath, he reined up the horse.

"Keep an eye peeled. Something is not right."

"Should I ring the alarm, Señor?"

"No sense waking everyone. I am going to check on the lookout posted on the east." He reined the horse around. "You hear any shots, sound the alarm."

"I will, Señor. I will."

Slocum set the leggy horse into a lope. Quickly he reached the position of the sentry, and no one was about in the starlight. From horseback, he searched around, wondering if the man was asleep somewhere close by. He hitched the horse to the vineyard, and had searched only a few feet of rows when he discovered a sandaled foot sticking out from under the vines.

Slocum's fist closed on the grip of his Colt. With care he glanced around and saw nothing, then bent over to examine the rest of the still body. When he used his arm to hold back the vegetation, he could see the man's throat was cut. He had been murdered and placed there by his killer. Slocum reached down and closed the dead guard's eyelids.

The man was cold to the touch, and had been dead long enough for his body's heat to escape. It meant the attack had come earlier. What did they want? Were they between him and the house, or had they fled? Damn, he should signal the guard at the gate. But it could be a false alarm. The killer could already be in the Madras.

Slocum rose and tried to think of his next move. He glanced at the ground. He must have stepped in the killer's tracks. Bent low, he tried to make out the tracks in the loose dirt. Then he saw the moccasin track. A one-piece sole didn't mean it was an *indio*. Lots of folks below the border made their own boots. Still, it wasn't Slocum's boot mark, nor the dead man's sandal.

Better get back to the main house. He undid the reins and spooked the horse in the process. He shied away. Slocum moved in, grasped the horn, made a jump for the stirrup, swung a leg over, found his seat, and caught up the horse as he boogered sideways down the row. When the horse was at last in check, he searched around.

Must be the copper smell of blood that made the horse so nervous, Slocum decided. The horse blew rollers out of his nose, and fled for the house when Slocum gave him the bit. Slocum pulled him down at the gate and looked for the guard overhead. Nothing. Some dogs barked down in the village.

A cold chill ran up the backs of his arms. He swung down, his fist full of the Colt's grip. Where was the man? In the shadows of the wall he knelt, and discovered the guard face-down. Dead or unconscious, Slocum wasn't certain. But the front doors of the house were standing wide open. He could see the gaping opening from where he knelt beside the fallen sentry.

Damn, were they in there already? How had he missed them? Maria! Hell, he'd never thought. El Lobo had come back for her. He rushed inside the front entrance, and his world went black. He was struck hard from behind, and the floor rushed up and met him.

"Señor? Señor?" a sobbing woman pleaded in his ear. He tried to open his lead-weighted eyelids. "They have taken Dona Maria. Oh, Señor, wake up, please?"

"Who did it?" he managed to ask with his cheek resting on the cool tile floor. Gingerly he reached back and discovered the raised knots on his scalp. Damn, they must have tried to cave in his skull.

"—Don't know who they were," the teary-voiced woman said. "Men have gone to find Franco. He is in the hills with the *vaqueros* rounding up the cattle."

"Oh, Señor," a man's voice from the door cried out. "They have killed poor Manuel. Cut his throat."

Slocum sat up, still holding his exploding head, and nodded. The man had spoken of the guard at the east side, the one Slocum had found earlier. "Anyone see them?"

"One was dressed as a *vaquero*—we think."

"Vaquero?" He remembered the smooth-soled track in the grape row. Lots of *vaqueros* wore high-top, home-made boots for protection from the thorns and cactus.

"Did he used to work here?"

"What do you mean, Señor?"

"A *vaquero* who once worked here gave Maria's identity away to that madam Lucinda. Maria never told me his name." The thunder inside his head roared so loud he held his hands to his ears. "He worked here—someone must know him."

"The only one that you could mean would be Tomas Morez," the woman said. She had returned with a pan of water and some cloths.

Slocum viewed the stone faces of the others who had filed in the hall and surrounded him.

"How is the guard outside?" he asked, sitting up, and she applied cool compresses to his sore head.

"He has a bad headache too and is sore, but he will live," one of the older men volunteered.

"Good." Slocum clasped his hands together and pressed them to his pounding forehead. What should he do? They would kill her so she could not be a witness against them.

He had one chance, that this Tomas and whoever was with him would take Maria to the madam in Nogales. If they went to the mountains instead, if they simply slit her throat in the desert . . . No way to know. He had to get his head right and there wasn't much time. Things were moving fast.

He forced himself to his feet, and a woman screamed when he staggered. It took great effort to straighten his back and catch his balance. He teetered on his boot heels, and waved away everyone's help.

"Saddle a horse. I need two men who can shoot to kill." He stared around the circle at their frightened faces.

"I will go with you." A man past forty with eyes dark as coals stepped forward.

"I will go."

Slocum saw the other volunteer from the corner of his eye. He twisted and nodded to the younger man. "We will ride some horses into the ground today. It is not a job for the faint of heart."

"The boy's name is Baca. The man," the woman said, and whirled to indicate him, "is Ferd."

"Good, Ferd, you and Baca go and get us three good horses saddled," Slocum said, and the two left on the run.

"Where are the guns?" he asked the woman from the kitchen.

"I will get some," she said. She hitched up her dress and hurried through the crowd.

"Shells too," he shouted after her. "There could be more bandits come here while I am gone. Bring in the guards at night. Use two men—" He pressed his hand to his forehead and tried to stem the explosions inside his skull. Damn, he must have Yankee cannons going off inside there. He opened his eyes, and the colors in the room had vanished. All he could see were the dark black and gray outlines of the hacienda people.

A baby cried in its mother's arms, and he tried to focus. How could he do anything feeling like this? Damn, maybe his vision would come back. Him and two farmhands against this Tomas and Lucinda. If that was where he took her. God, let her be there and don't let them hurt her.

"The horses are ready," Ferd said, taking two pistols from the woman. Then she gave a holster to the boy, Baca, who swung it around his waist as if he had worn one before. With some show of expertise, he loaded and holstered the Colt she handed him.

Slocum felt satisfied the men knew handguns. All he could see was black and white. His head pounded away with volley after volley going off inside his skull. He led the way outside, made two tries to mount the skittish fresh horse, and at last managed to get in the saddle. They charged out the gate and down the lane. Their ponies would be spent or wind-broke by the time they reached Nogales. He hoped he didn't get too dizzy to stay in the saddle.

He rode with the wind sweeping his bleary eyes. They reached Nogales on lathered, out-of-wind horses, and he asked a boy on the street the location of Lucinda's place. With his directions, they rode their head-hung, snorting horses up the street.

"We will go in the front or the back?" Ferd asked.

"You and Baca come in the back door. Bust it in when you hear me come in the front one. If they've got a gun in their hand, shoot them first before they shoot you, un-less they have her as a hostage."

"You all right?" the man asked.

"Fine," Slocum lied. His vision came and went. It grew darker, and then had periods when he saw good enough, but he still saw no color. He hoped when he kicked in that front door, it was during one of the better times. At the moment, he could hardly make out the building fronts they rode past, let alone an individual with a gun in his hand. Hell, if they hurt her . . .

"That's the whorehouse." Ferd pointed to the building.

Slocum agreed. He dropped from the saddle, hoping his legs worked. All he could see was the outline of the build-ing. Forced to take the man's word, he lifted the .45 out of the holster and decided it was free enough to draw.

"I can go with you," Ferd said.

"No, you and Baca be certain this Tomas don't get away."

"You really all right, Señor?" the boy finally asked.

"Bueno, Baca, bueno." He tried to stand more upright, and knew he wasn't steady in his walk. "Go around back." He waved them in that direction.

They reined their horses away, but he could tell they were uncertain about him. Damn, how much further was this building? A half a block. He must have dismounted that far from it, for the outline kept growing bigger. Then his boot toe struck a step and his hand shot out for the railing. He mounted the stairs and headed for—no, that was a window.

At last he stood before the curtained glass pane of the door. He drew the Colt, and raised his boot up and smashed it hard against the side beside the knob. It didn't open, and he did it again. This time the glass shattered in the window and fell noisily in shards inside and out. He tried the knob, and it opened in his hand. Damn.

He looked up and saw someone at the second-story railing. A gun blasted and splinters exploded in his face from the door casing, which sent him diving inside on the polished floor. Behind a sofa on his belly, he tried to get his bearings and hear enough to tell where he must aim at to get the shooter.

Women began screaming and cussing. Hell, was Maria even in the building? She must be, or why else did they shoot at him? Was he too late? If he could only see. Lord, just give him a glimpse of this madman. It was all he wanted.

More shots came from the back of the house. Wouldn't do a bit of good for him to look up, the little he could see. He shook his head in defeat and squeezed his eyelids tight shut.

"Señor Slocum?" Ferd called to him.

"Yes?" He rose on his elbows.

"One man is dead."

"Have you found her?"

"No, not back there."

Filled with dread, he rose to his feet. "Tomas is dead?"

"No, Señor, another man. He is the one who shot at you."

"Shit. What else is going to happen?" Slocum tried to focus his eyes. They still did not work. "Baca, you tear this damn place apart. If she's here, find her."

"You'll do no such thing, Who in the hell do you think you are?" a large-framed woman demanded, coming down the stairs. He could make out enough of her outline. She must be Lucinda.

"Lady, you get in the way, I'll blow daylight through you where they can drive a damn wagon through. Where's she at?"

"I'll have the police—"

"No, where is Maria Obregon?"

"She's certainly not here."

"Baca, search the damn rooms upstairs." He gave a wave with his gun hand.

"Just a minute—"

Slocum shoved her roughly aside, and the boy tore up the stairs.

"She better be alive." He waved the muzzle close to her face. Then he felt a wave of dizziness coming on and searched for a place to sit down.

"I have powerful friends," she said.

"Is that dead one in back the same one who sold her to Montrose?" He sat down on the sofa and closed his eyes. His stomach roiled to go with his headaches and the swarming feeling in his head.

"I have no idea who you have murdered. And I know of no Montrose."

"He wasn't worth much. How much did you pay Tomas to kidnap her?"

"I don't have to answer your absurd questions—"

"Slocum! Slocum! She's up here," Baca shouted from the balcony.

Alive or dead? He closed his eyes and his shoulders slumped in dread.

13

"He may never see again," the man's voice said in Spanish.

Under the bandages over his eyes, Slocum could hear the words. The laudanum he'd taken earlier had stopped the hurting, but it made everything feel and sound miles away from him.

"Can't tell much about a brain injury. One bad enough to affect his vision, it could be permanent. Make him keep the bandages on for two weeks. I'll come by and check on him."

"*Gracias*, Doctor," Maria said, and Slocum heard the door close after the man.

He felt her fingers intertwine with his.

"Rest easy," she said in English. "I'll find a better doctor for you. Maybe go to Tucson. Don't worry, Slocum. Tomorrow they are bringing a rig from the hacienda with a bed in it to take you there. This woman, Millie, thinks you would be safer out there.

"I knew you were downstairs when I heard the glass shatter." Her fingers tightened on his. "Oh, I just knew they had killed you, Slocum, when Tomas took me from ranch. But at that woman's place, when that windowpane shattered and she gave a scream, I knew it was you. I didn't know if it was you or your ghost, but I knew you had come to rescue me."

"Ferd and Baca," he said in a raspy weak whisper that shocked even himself.

"They told me all about you. Blind and all, you still kicked in the door. Why, you could have been killed. Slocum, those men that are after you, I promise you that they will never take you from my hacienda. Those bounty hunters—the ranch people won't ever let them do that."

He nodded to signify he'd heard her words. Without eyes, he couldn't survive long. Maybe for a short while, but greed would send some killers, and how would he see them coming? Who had lit the match that night? He had heard that the dead man in the whorehouse was Gerald, the one who had originally sold Maria to Montrose. Lucinda was in jail awaiting her trial. Except for the fact that Tomas had escaped and was not to be found, the matter was settled.

Didn't she say earlier that Bollinsky was coming to see him? Good, even if he couldn't see the captain. One of them had some vision anyway. He shivered under the cover despite the day's heat. He recalled an old blind slave he had known back in Georgia. The man used neat's-foot oil on all his master's leather goods. His thumbs rubbed in the precious liquid hour after hour to preserve the saddles, bridle, harness.

Maybe they needed someone to oil leather at her hacienda. But to never see a sunrise—laudanum-induced sleep took him away.

He awoke on top of a shaking bed to the sound of iron rims rolling over the hard ground. A canvas cover over the wagon must be shading him some from the sun's rays. How long had he slept? He'd never even known when they transported him, bed and all, to the rig. He could hear men riding horses beside it. No doubt armed with rifles, the *vaqueros* must be ready to repel an army on his behalf.

"You awake?" Maria asked, and moved in to take his hand.

"Yes. How far are we from the hacienda?" he asked, confused by his blindness and a growing impatience.

"Oh, a few hours and we will be there. I told them it was no race."

"Good," he said, being rocked back and forth in the wagon. His mouth tasted dry as cotton, and the nagging headache returned to his temples. It would be hard for him to live this dark life, blind and helpless.

"Take some more medicine," she said.

He shook his head. It only made him groggy and dull-minded. He hated the wasted feeling that the painkiller gave him. No, he would try to tough this day out. Maybe it was morning? No telling what time it was. If things didn't start happening for the better—why did he harbor this small voice that told him the end of his life was near? He could visualize himself walking around blind and accidentally stepping off into a thousand-foot chasm.

No, he would see again. But what if he only had partial vision? Black and white, like before. He would not survive long in any case. Once the Abbott brothers knew he was sightless, they would swarm him like buzzards at a hog killing. Circle around until they found a chance to gun him down. Then he would be planted in some isolated boot hill grown up in bunch grass.

He managed with Maria's help to get out of the bed when they reached the hacienda. Light-headed, he hobbled along with her under his arm for a crutch into the coolness of the great house. Then, a step at a time, she eased him upstairs. By the time they reached her feather bed, he was exhausted. He fell on the bed and slept.

It was sometime later when he felt her supple body

molded to his and heard a small voice in his ear. "You hungry?"

"For what?" he asked, and despite the drum in his head, her sweet musk ran up his nose and tickled the nerve endings inside his skull.

"Food, silly. Or—"

"Yes, let's or," he said, and ran his hand over her bare leg.

"I don't want to hurt you."

"Too far from my eyes to hurt me."

"I wasn't sure, but I missed you." She snuggled closer.

"I missed you," he said, and cupped her left breast in his hand. He felt the silky skin and growing hardness of the knobby nipple under the center of his palm. He closed his eyes and rubbed the flat muscles of her belly, until he found the triangle of coarse hair. Then his fingers slipped into the seam and she rolled over on her back.

With the tip of his finger he traced down the canyon, testing the still-unawake peak of her womanhood, then went deeper until his probe could search the gate. It was well lubricated, and he had only traced around the outside when her legs widened and her hips rose for more. He tested the ring of fire, and felt her grasp the sheet in her fingers.

In another second, he gently probed, teasing and twisting his finger only a short ways inside her. Soon her hand clutched the top of his and drove him deeper. Her back arched to accept all of it. She moaned in the throes of pleasure.

"Do it," she cried. "Now!"

He rose up light-headed on his hands and knees to obey her. He was uncertain that he could even stand the strain, but the rock-hard shaft between his legs throbbed with his need for her. His hips ached to pound it into her. Raw desire filled his sore brain with an insatiable appetite to plunge in her.

She gave a small scream when he poked the head into her lubricated gate. Contracting muscular walls tried to exclude and expel him, but the force of his pile-driving butt soon won the war. Her fingernails clawed his back, and soon their bodies became welded together into one humping force.

He felt the charge coming from deep in his testicles, and when it shot into her depths, the last strand of energy left him like a broken violin string. Drained, he melted into a pile, and somehow she eased him off her. The last thing he heard before he fell asleep was, "Don't you want some food?"

At the end of the week, the doctor came out to the ranch. Slocum heard him and Maria talking Spanish in the hallway. He sat up in the bed, tried to clear his groggy brain, and waited.

"How are you today, my son?" the doctor asked, entering the room.

"All right."

"Oh, can you see any light behind the bandage?"

"Not much."

The physician began to unwind the bandage from his head. "I had hoped by now you would see some light anyway."

"Pretty dark."

"I understand. I want to look in the eyes and see."

Some light did enter his eyes once the bandage was removed, but it was still like inky night. He could see the shadow of the doctor's hand when it came close to him. When it was near enough, he could feel the wind of it moving by.

"Can you see any light at all?"

"Some."

"I thought by now you would be more improved." The man made a creaking sound beside the bed when he took the chair. "I am afraid there is nothing else I can do for you."

"Is there anyone?" Maria asked. "Any doctor you might recommend that we go see?"

"No, I am truly sorry, Señorita, but I fear his vision is lost. Maybe in time. We know so little about the brain." The man sounded completely baffled by Slocum's condition.

"I must go," he said hurriedly, and the chair gave a groan of relief that Slocum heard. "I have left you plenty of laudanum, though she says you seldom take it. It won't fix your eyes, only ease the suffering."

"*Gracias,*" Slocum said.

"God be with you, my son," the man said, and Slocum listened to Maria and him talk. Something about a doctor in Tucson.

"Slocum?" she asked, coming back in the room. He felt her presence when she took the chair and reached for his hand. She kissed his fingers. "What do you want to do?"

"Find a witch."

"A witch? But Dr. Mendese is the best physician around. What could a witch do?"

"Your people used witches for centuries before doctors were even invented. They cured lots of things. Have Franco find me a good one."

"Oh, Slocum—" She kissed him on the mouth. "I can't let some witch cast a spell on you."

"Not a spell. A cure."

"I'll do as you ask, but I can't be responsible for the results. Witches do crazy things. Would you not try the doctors in Tucson?"

"A witch," he said again.

"A witch it will be. But I don't—I don't like it."

He never answered her. A sorceress was the best approach he could think of for his plight. Maria might not trust them, but he had no choice but to put his faith in one, since the medical doctor said he had no cures for his condition.

"I will get more than one," she said. "Then if one of them is playing tricks on you, the other ones will know and I can stop her."

"Good," he grunted, and rolled over to sleep some more.

The day passed, and another. He began to believe there were no witches in all of northern Sonora. The next day they came, or rather, Maria brought them in one at a time to see him.

"This is Bonita," Maria said. "Señor Slocum."

He sat up on the bed and listened to the sounds of Bonita's bare feet on the tile. Her clothing made a soft swish like silk, and she smelled of sage smoke. He wondered if she was old or young. He felt her callused fingers open each eye to inspect them. Her thin fingers felt like hard sticks and were powerful to the touch.

"You see no light?" she asked.

"I only see your shadow," he said.

She breathed through her nose, then swung something about her dress back over her shoulder. He felt her move away as if appraising him.

"I know of a medicine that might help. It cured a *vaquero* once who was thrown from his horse and hit his head on a boulder." She paused. "He could see nothing but shadows. I must go make the medicine. Maybe if I find it quickly I will return in two days, Señor."

"Gracias, Bonita."

"I will show her out," Maria said.

He agreed and slumped down. She had once cured a *vaquero* with a similar condition. Would it work on him?

"This is Bayonkia," Maria announced. "His name is Slocum."

The woman's sandals slapped the tile and she hurriedly

circled him and the bed. While she did so, she cleared her throat. "They say you see nothing. Raise your head and look at me. Ah, do you see anything?"

"Light, and close enough I can see your shadow."

Her hands began to explore his skull. She felt the knots from the blows. Then she blew her breath in each eye. It was not unpleasant, but he wondered about her purpose.

"They must have hit you very hard?"

"I was out for some time."

"Then you saw some," Maria declared.

"Yes, enough to ride to town, but never very good."

"Hmm, what did the doctors give you?" the witch asked.

"Laudanum."

"You don't hurt, do you?"

"He hasn't taken any in three days," Maria said. "It made him too groggy, he said."

"I would think so. Give him some willow bark tea three or four times a day. That will help the headaches. You have headaches, don't you?"

"Yes."

"Slocum, you never said—" Maria scolded him.

"He is a tough man," Bayonkia said. "Oh, he has headaches and bad ones."

"How could you tell?" he asked.

"I see it in your eyes, but while they don't see me, they don't look damaged. That damage is inside your head."

"What can you do for it?" Maria asked.

The woman did not answer Maria's question for a long moment. Then she began. "The medicine might make him worse. I am not certain."

"What is it?" Slocum asked.

"Herbs I have gathered."

"Why would you give it then?" he asked.

"It is all that I know that might work."

"Would you take it in my place?" he asked.

"*Sí,*" she said quickly.

"Wait," Maria cautioned him. "There is one more medicine woman in the hall. I want to have her look at you first."

"As you say. But don't wait too long," Bayonkia warned sternly.

"We won't," Maria said, and he listened to their footsteps go toward the hallway.

In a short while, he heard someone return and smelled the pungent smoke of sage. He wondered what was happening when Maria explained, "This is Sophie. She has incense that she burns to chase away the evil."

He visualized some woman swinging a brass container on a gold chain that contained the sage, and the smokelike streamers filling the room. While she walked about, she also chanted in a strange language he had never heard.

"The smoke will help you. Have they sweated you?" she asked.

"No."

"You should be in a sweat lodge. The darkness would help and the right vapors could heal you."

"Has this worked on others?" Maria asked.

"Always helps. Opens the pores, lets the poison out. He will never be well without a three-day sweat bath. Night and day. There must be plenty of steam."

"We could try that," Maria said out loud.

"It would help him."

"Turn me into a wrinkled fig," was all that Slocum could think. Three days in a sweat lodge would be long-term torture, not treatment. Maria didn't trust those other women's medicine—why did she sound so interested in this method? He wasn't certain the sweat lodge might not kill him too.

Sophie left, and Maria came to sit beside him.

"Who did you believe we should use?" she asked.

"Bayonkia."

"But she warned you—"

"I'll take the chance."

"Slocum, if it becomes worse—I don't know what I will do."

"Maria, it is bad now. I mean, I have to listen to things to know when people are in the room. I can't hardly tell the time of day or night."

"I'll go tell her to make her medicine."

Slocum agreed, and used his hands to clamp his pounding temples. The roar increased and the beat grew stronger every hour he was awake. Let the witch's medicine work—please.

"And I'll bring back some willow bark tea too," Maria said.

Good. Maybe something the woman had in her medicine bag would work. He had no other options.

14

"This will taste bad," Bayonkia warned him. "And you may become delirious."

"What will it do to me?" he asked.

"I am not certain. Some who have taken it get very upset."

"Will I hurt anyone?"

She didn't answer.

"I don't want to hurt you or anyone," Slocum said.

"I don't think you will, but you must promise to return."

"Return?" Maria asked in a small voice. "What if he can't?"

"I don't know."

"Maria, it will be all right," he said to reassure her. "Let's get it done."

The thick liquid tasted chalky at first when he sipped from the cup Bayonkia handed him. Then the bitterness grew stronger. He forced himself to swallow, but it threatened to reverse in his throat. He fought the urges to vomit, and kept drinking more of it from the vessel she held to his mouth.

"Ugh," he said at last, and wiped his mouth on the back

of his hand. Fumes of it began to assail his nose. He felt himself go limp, and the two women assisted him back on the bed.

"He is fine," Bayonkia said to Maria. "We must stand back and let it work—"

Flames began to consume his mind. Trapped by them, he began to run through the spaces that were still not ablaze. The heat he expected was strangely not there. In his race to find some escape and a place of safety, he began to wonder if there was any end to this inferno. His breath remained good and his legs showed no sign of fading. He leaped through a small channel between the soaring orange-red tongues towering twice his height.

His feet now on a smooth surface, he ran uphill, crossing another line of the flames. He slowed to catch his breath, and then he hurried on as though his destination must be further away. At last he stood on the edge of a sheer precipice. Hundreds of feet below his boot toes, a cauldron of boiling green mud belched and churned.

Flames grew hotter and licked at him, narrowing the room left to stand. The spaces between the rows of fire closed in. Even the air grew thinner. When there was no way to go back, he leaped off the ledge and settled in for the next trial.

He hit feet-first and splashed the liquid high. Then, using his swimming skills to emerge, he began to dog-paddle in the current sweeping him away. The sulphurous taste of the mud in his mouth made his tongue curl, and he tried to spit it out.

On each side, he could see people standing on the bank in the mist, and they laughed at him. Men that he had known, like Montrose—the sight of his grizzly-bear face and raucous laughter made Slocum's blood boil. Then he saw others, all outlaws. Brocious Bill from Tombstone. His great hulk was like some Chinese statue of Buddha dressed in a breechcloth. Brocious was laughing at his plight. A renegade Apache—no, it was Geronimo who stood on the shores and did a war dance to celebrate Slocum's fate. The chief dropped his loincloth and stepped out of it. Then he turned around and mooned Slocum with his bare brown ass as they often did when they knew they were beyond the range of the soldiers' rifles.

Soon the mud became a frothy mill stream, and Slocum found himself on foot amid a stampede of cattle. Lightning danced off a thousand longhorns and turned the night blue with the eerie light. The same sulphurous smell that he first recalled returned. He climbed on a steer and rose to his feet, then ran across the steers' backs.

How many times had he rode at breakneck speed to stop such a stampede? Thundering hooves, the bawl of ten thousand steers on the move—all of it was in his ears. He jumped from back to back, catching his balance and going on. How many cowboys did he bury in the next morning's light? Good men, like Shorty Hurne, Billy Gail, Thurman, and Hank, to name a few of the top hands. Using his outflung arms to steady himself, he danced on the steers' backs in the night's blackness. There had to be an end to them. A place to get off.

Then he saw the woman emerge from an opening of blue light. She wore a gauzy white dress and stood seven feet tall. Her voluptuous body took his breath away.

"Slocum," she called in a wavering voice. "I need you."

He tried to steady himself, standing on the back of two galloping steers. Who was she? An angel? He blinked his pained eyes when she pulled away the cloth on her shoulders. His heart began to thump like a mule kicking under his breastbone. Then she undid the blouse and slowly exposed her long firm breasts. The white silky material fluttered away from her fingertips.

"Slocum, Slocum," she called over the stampede's loud noises. "I need you."

He watched her untie the belted ribbons at her waist.

He waited, standing on his rolling platform. His legs felt filled with lead, and his eyes refused to look away from her, as if they were welded on her, as she deftly picked at the strands until he could see that they were free and the lacy skirt was swept away by the wind.

Her blue eyes drilled holes in him. Her left hand slid over the ivory skin on her flat stomach, and then she cupped the dark triangle above her stemlike legs. The other hand beckoned him to come to her.

Her voice grew sweeter. "Oh, Slocum, I need you so much."

She pursed her full red lips at him as if in pain. Her blue eyes narrowed and they pleaded. The reaction in his pants grew rock hard. She began to dance. Her long hips were gyrating and her hands waving like willow boughs in a gentle wind.

Gawdamn, he wanted her. She sure wanted him. He tore his gaze away from her and looked over the backs of the thundering cattle. What had the witch said? Bayonkia's words grew louder in his ears, even over the deafening roar of the stampeding herd and all those cattle crying out in the confusion and pain.

"You must come back."

When he looked over his shoulder again, he saw the light of dawn barely creasing the horizon. He could hear the woman's pleading calls to him.

"Slocum, you and I, we can make love forever. Come to me now before it's too late. Slocum, please . . ."

Too late? He didn't dare turn back to look at her.

"Slocum, please come to me—" She sounded further away.

The whole herd slowed down. He realized his future definitely could not be with her. Still, he fought the urge to take one last look at her magnificent body. He kept his gaze locked on the emerging sunrise and the line of golden light filling the horizon. What was wrong? He thought that direction was west. She had come up in the east. There was not a star in the sky when he searched for them overhead. Where was he anyway?

"Damn you!" she screeched in angry rage. "I'll teach you to scorn me!" A fierce bolt of lightning struck the ground beside him, killing the steers he stood on and a hundred more. Blinded by the flash, he found himself scrambling to escape from among the sea of dead and dying cattle. Flying horns and flailing hooves flashed by his face. Still, no matter how hard he fought and tried, he couldn't get to his feet.

"Let me up, dammit!" he swore out loud. Somehow he must get out of there.

15

"Slocum, are you all right?"

He looked up into the sweat-streaked faces of Maria and a swarthy-complected woman. Each held him down with both hands pressed hard on his shoulders. He blinked his sore eyes at them, and he could still see them. The colors in their dresses sparkled red, green, blue.

"Bayonkia?" he asked.

"Yes." A sly smile sliced her dark thin lips. "Do I look as you supposed that I would?"

"You two look better than angels. I saw one of them, or the devil's handmaiden, a few minutes ago."

"You can see?" Maria swallowed hard. "What did the angel look like?"

"Tall—she was no angel. I need a drink of water badly."

Bayonkia helped him to a sitting position while Maria fumbled to pour him a drink.

"Can you still see?" Maria asked, rushing back with the pottery cup.

"See good. Bright in here, though." He closed his eyes against the glare.

"Your eyes will adjust to the light in time," said Bayonkia. "It is not bright in here. You should wear colored goggles for a few weeks outside."

"Those red-lens things that dudes wear?" He looked at the witch in disapproval.

"Yes, they will help."

He took the water and quickly drank it. Might take a whole well to satisfy him. His shirt and britches felt clammy—he must have been in a big sweat during that treatment. Maria's hair was matted on her forehead. "You have a rough time holding me down the whole time?" he asked her.

"You were a handful at the end is all," she said, and swiped her bangs back.

"It didn't last long, did it?"

"You took the potion this morning. It is almost six o'clock now," Maria said with a smile.

"That long?" Slocum could hardly believe them. Strange, his head didn't hurt. No headache.

"I need to go find the facilities," he said, and pushed off his knees.

"You sure you can make it?" Maria asked, concerned, checking with Bayonkia.

"I'll be fine, if some seven-foot-tall witch don't get me." He looked at the two women, who appeared in shock at his words. "What is wrong with you two?"

"You're describing the medicine woman they call Bonita."

"She wear a gauzy white dress?"

"Oh, yes, a beautiful woman."

"It wasn't her," he lied, and headed for the doorway. "I never saw her in person."

"You sure described her perfectly. She had what color eyes?"

"Blue," he said absently over his shoulder.

"Slocum! Where did you see her?" Maria shouted after him.

"In those damn wild dreams Bayonkia gave me," he said with a shake of his head, and went on. Crazy coincidence was all. He nodded to one of the kitchen girls going by, and she looked at him wide-eyed.

"Señor, you can see again?"

"Oh, yes."

"Madre de Dios!" She ran off screaming about a miracle.

It was a miracle or a witch's spell. Still, he wished he had seen that Amazon witch in real life. He made his way outside to the privy. It felt good to vent his bladder again. Seeing the hard stream disappear into the dark oval hole made him feel much better. He hoped that all that medicine ran out with it. He didn't need another experience like that one, no matter if it did restore his vision.

With a wide-brim straw hat and red goggles, he rode with Franco across the desert to check on the river water. At this time of year, every eye on the hacienda watched for the monsoon rains to sweep in off the Gulf of California and water their thirsty land.

"You have no word of this Tomas?" Slocum asked the man.

"No one has heard of him since he delivered Maria to that woman's house."

"He can't just vanish unless someone killed him."

"There are many men on this hacienda that would love to do just that to him. Maybe first they would nail his balls to a board."

"Use rusty nails too, I suppose?"

"Ah, *sí.*"

"And El Lobo still eludes the *rurales.*"

"But the captain, he is trying hard to catch him."

"I know he is very serious. Good thing that Montrose and Wilton are in jail." Slocum glanced over at the man when he did not reply. "They are in jail, aren't they?"

"No, Señor, they escaped the jail while you were so sick. I didn't want you to worry about them."

"What do you people have jails for down here?"

Franco made a pained face. "In Mexico, many times it is why the law, they don't bring them in alive."

Slocum better understood Bollinsky's actions in the mountains. He twisted in the saddle to view their back-trail, and studied the burned-up desert behind them. Even the greasewood looked drab in the sea of straw-brown grass. A soaking rain would be extra nice. He pulled down the hat brim against the sun and rode on.

In the late afternoon of the next day, he cleaned his hand-guns on the big table in the great room. He took the small .30-caliber six-gun from his boot, and with his fingers and a rag, he worked freshly boiled oil over the metal surfaces. A man never knew when an extra bullet might be needed. He reassembled the weapon, then loaded each cylinder with powder and lead. For a close-up gun, the .30 was a dandy. He capped five of them, let the hammer rest on the sixth one.

He pulled up his pants leg and restored the small revolver to its place. Maria came from the front.

"A man to see you. Won't talk to me."

"You know him?"

"No, but he wants to talk to you."

"I better go see. He look tough?" When she shook her head, he headed for the front door.

She followed him.

"Good afternoon," he said to the man on the burro. He looked like a simple unarmed *peon*.

"Are you Slocum?"

"They call me that. What do you have for me?"

The man was in his twenties, Slocum guessed. He looked all around before he spoke to be certain that they were alone.

"They said you would pay a big reward to know where a man called Tomas Morez was hiding."

"Who told you that?"

"A bartender in San Felipe."

"He told you right. Do you know Tomas?"

The man shook his head. "But I heard Tomas's brother say that Tomas was hiding at Harlequin in Arizona."

"Was his brother drunk?" Slocum asked.

"Of course. That is why I know that it is the truth."

"What did they say the reward would be?"

The man shrugged.

"Is ten pesos enough?"

The man jerked off his hat. "Plenty, Don Slocum."

Slocum smiled at his words. He dug out the coins and tossed them into the man's outstretched hat.

"Gracias, Señor." His coins secure, the man replaced his sombrero and chin strap, then rode off on his donkey.

"What will you do about Tomas?" Maria asked quietly beside him.

"What do you think I will do?" he asked her. "I aim to go find him."

"Not by yourself?"

"Maybe take the boy Baca along to hold the horses."

"You should take several of my men with you up there."

"No, they have work here. Besides, with all these killers out of jail, I want you to have a strong force here should anything happen."

"You will leave before the rooster crows, right?" She took his arm.

"Probably."

"Then we must go at once to my room."

"I have things to pack—"

"Oh, no. I come first."

He looked at the clear azure sky. His eyes were stronger. Well, she wasn't half bad to look at now that he could see her again. So he put off his leaving a little longer.

She slipped under his arm and held his hand. "You never told me everything about that woman Millie."

"You met her." He glanced down and frowned at the top of her head.

"She said you were friends in Kansas."

"Maria, that was so long ago I plumb forgot."

She elbowed him in the ribs. "I doubt that." And they went inside the house.

He thought about this place called Harlequin over on the Arizona side of the line. A robber's roost, with some small mines in the area. Worthless riffraff hung out there. The hangout straddled the international border between Nogales and Ft. Huahucha.

"Did you live with her for long in Kansas?" Maria insisted, crossing the great room.

"Who?"

"Millie?"

"Lord, no."

"Slocum, why do I think you are lying?"

"Damned if I know," he said, and hugged her shoulder. Women could find the damnedest subjects to dwell on. Harlequin and the kidnapper filled his thoughts. Maybe in a few days he would have answers.

She closed and barred the bedroom door behind them. Still deep in his own thoughts, he toed off his left boot and watched her undress. He wrinkled his nose at the thought of the seven-foot-tall siren. Maria's shapely five-foot body was enough for him. Damn, Tomas Morez was hiding out at Harlequin. He planned to be there in a few days.

16

Dressed in the unbleached cotton clothing of a *peon*, with a well-worn tattered-edge serape and a Chihuahua-shaped dirty straw hat, Slocum rode a skinny red roan horse. He and Baca reined up their mustangs short of the town of Harlequin and studied the situation.

Nestled in some craggy foothills with plenty of bushy junipers, and lots of well-used mining equipment scattered about rusting away, the town looked like little more than a smattering of shacks that clung on the two hillsides, with the gray-weathered wood-sided business establishments clustered next to the narrow wagon road that wound out of the north and ran into Sonora behind their backs. Most of the stores were boarded up, an obvious sign that things were on the wane in this place.

Slocum stopped before the open store. The previous owner's name had been crossed out, and another painted on the board in fresh white letters. Teller's. He paused. Where had he heard that name before? Was this Imogene's father? He dried his palms on the dirt-streaked front of his once-white pants. Maybe he needed to go in there and castrate the old man if it was actually him.

He motioned for Baca to stay with the horses, and slipped off his roan.

"I won't be long. I need to check on this." He looked up and down the empty wagon tracks, with the ribbon of sun-cured grass in the center, that served as a street. He saw nothing out of place. Then he hitched up his baggy pants and went inside the front door.

A bell rang over his head, and a whiskered man in a rocker nodded at him.

"Good afternoon," Slocum said in Spanish.

"Same to you, greaser," the old man grumbled.

"I bet you're from Texas," Slocum said.

"Yeah. Wish to hell I'd never left there. Lost my wife and my oldest daughter to damn gyp-water poisoning coming out here. Got me one left, though. Lacey, honey, come in here and wait on this greaser."

A slender girl of perhaps fourteen came into the store from the living quarters in back. She would not make eye contact with Slocum.

"What do you need?" she asked. With her head down and her arms folded over her budding chest, she waited for him to tell her what he needed.

"Some matches," Slocum said, recalling his role as a *peon*.

"Be two cents," she said, and put the box on the counter.

Before he left Harlequin, he would take her away from this old goat. There was little doubt he was using her the way he had used her older sister Imogene. *Millie, you'll have one more stray to care for.*

"Gracias," he said, and paid her and took the matches.

"You need some work, boy?" Teller asked.

At the door, Slocum turned and looked back at the old man.

"They need some hands up at the Fredrick mine. Take the second road to the left. Tell Bart I sent you, boy. He'll be grateful. You look like you need some work."

Slocum nodded. He noted that the girl stood with her back to the shelves behind the counter. No telling what that old boar had subjected her to already. After he found Tomas, he planned to come back for her. With a sharp pang of conscience for leaving her there, he went out the door with the ringing bell.

"What did you buy?" Baca asked, leaning down.

"Matches," Slocum said in a low tone.

"We need them?"

"No, but I needed an excuse to buy something. There is a man in there that sleeps with his own daughters."

"Are you sure?"

"Positive."

"Who is he?"

"Name's right here on the sign. Teller." Slocum pointed to it.

"How did you know him?"

"Met his oldest daughter a month ago. She works for a friend of mine in Nogales. She told me everything about him."

"What are we going to do about him?" Baca made a cold face at the notion of incest.

Slocum nodded at him to reassure him. "We'll do something sure enough, after we find Tomas."

"I am with you, Slocum." The youth drew his horse's head up from grazing with both hands on the reins.

"I know you are," Slocum said, and booted his horse away from the storefront.

Down the road, they found a blacksmith, busy drawing out steel, and Slocum dismounted to talk to the man. The ring of his hammer was pealing off through the morning air. He looked up. Beads of sweat raced down the man's deeply tanned face. His bare arms bulged with muscles and his hairy chest looked like that of a buffalo.

"Morning, strangers." The man took a break from his coal-fired forge and the hammer.

"Morning, yourself," Slocum said with a sharp nod. "You know of a *vaquero* around here who's called Tomas?"

"I know Tomas. He lives up that hill in the red cabin."

"Thanks." Slocum glanced at the juniper-dotted hill, and though he could see the rusty red cabin.

"No problem. You two have business to do here?"

"No, just passing through and needed to see Tomas."

"He should be up there. I ain't seen him ride by all day."

"Gracias," Slocum said, recalling his disguise again.

The wagon tracks up the hill were dim. A single path threaded its way through the dimmer road, worn to the dirt, and rocks showed travel by a single horse and people probably afoot.

"He recognizes you, he may run or go for a gun," Slocum warned the boy.

"Want me to stay back?"

"Yes. I might fool him. Wait here. You hear shots, come a-spurring."

Baca stayed back, and Slocum pushed the roan up the trail. He rounded a tall thick stand of junipers and spotted the dull red cabin. Smoke rose from the rusted chimney pipe. Tomas, or whoever was inside, must be cooking something. Slocum rode up to the porch. The steps were broken, and several boards in the porch looked rotted.

"What do you need, hombre?" A short Mexican came to the doorway and rolled himself a cigarette with corn shucks.

"I am looking for a ranch hand. You Tomas?"

"Who is it?" a woman's voice asked from inside in Spanish.

"Someone who wants a *vaquero*," the man said, busy rolling the smoke with both hands. When he looked up from his task, he blinked in disbelief at the Colt in Slocum's hand.

"Put your hands in the air." Slocum turned the roan, then with care stepped off onto the porch with the muzzle still pointed at the man. "Who is here?"

"Ramona." Hands held high, Tomas nodded toward the house.

"Where is Montrose?"

The man shrugged. "I don't know no Montrose."

Slocum jerked the cap-and-ball pistol from the man's holster and the big frog-sticker from the scabbard behind his back. He shoved him inside the room.

"No reason to panic," he said to the young woman standing at the stove. Then he stuck his head out the door and shouted for Baca to come on.

"Baca—" Tomas's dark eyes showed his concern, and he looked hard at Slocum. "You are from the hacienda?"

"That's right."

"What will you do with my Tomas?" Ramona cried out, and began to dry her hands on the apron.

"Probably string him up. He knew that Maria Obregon was a prisoner at Lucinda's whorehouse and never told the law. Then he kidnapped her and took her back there so they could kill her."

"He never did that!"

"Sorry, but Maria Obregon will testify he did that to her."

"Oh, no." The woman began to cry.

Baca came in the room and frowned at Slocum. "He didn't want to go for his gun?"

"Never gave him a chance. Get a rope and tie him up. Ramona is cooking our breakfast."

She blinked at Slocum with her wet eyelashes, then went back to the stove to save her food from burning.

"I have some money. I could pay you," Tomas offered.

"Give it to Ramona, she'll need it," Slocum said. "Baca, take it from him. He had no plans to do it that way."

The *vaquero*'s eyes turned black as coal. Slocum sat down at the table while Baca searched Tomas and put a handful of money in front of Slocum.

With care, Baca straightened out the folded ten-dollar bills and laid them in a stack. Kidnapping Maria must have paid very well. Slocum counted nearly a hundred dollars American.

"Ramona, you will be very rich with all this money when we ride out," Slocum said. "But if you go to Sonora and buy this no-good out of jail, I will return and you too will sit in the calaboose for a very long time. Do you savvy?"

"He said he had no money." She frowned with concern at Slocum.

Slocum played a hunch. "Did he tell you about his wife and children he left at the hacienda?"

"No." She looked in disbelief at Tomas.

Baca never said a word. He stacked the silver coins on the table.

"He lies," Tomas said. "Don't believe this gringo."

"No, *he* lies. Her name is Rosa," Baca said without looking up.

"I was going to tell you—" Tomas strained his bound up arms at the ropes. "I will kill the both of you! I swear on my mother's grave I will."

"You lied about Rosa. You kidnapped Maria Obregon. Now who in the hell is going to believe you? Sit there and shut up or I'll gag you." Slocum looked at the dishes of eggs and browned pork Ramona served to him and Baca.

"We can deal with Tomas later," Slocum told his sidekick. "It is time to eat this wonderful food that Ramona has fixed for us, amigo." She beamed at him, sticking her well-endowed chest out.

"You want more, Ramona will fix you some more," she said.

"What will you do now that you are rich, Ramona?" Slocum asked between bites of the hot, spicy food.

"Go back to Nogales."

"And what will you do there?" The tasty pork caused the saliva to flood into his mouth.

"Work in a whorehouse where I found her," Tomas said sarcastically from his place seated on the floor.

"So you wish," she said, and turned away from him. "I am going to open a dress shop. I can sew and all those *putas* need fancy dresses. I will hire some girls to help me."

"Don't bail this worthless one out," Slocum reminded her. "You will become a rich lady with that dress store." He motioned for her to take the money.

She quickly stuffed the money between her deep cleavage. Then she straightened and smiled at Slocum. "I will make you some nice shirts too. Come see me."

"I will," he promised. "Very good food.

"Can you take the prisoner back to the ranch?" he asked Baca.

Slocum wanted him to turn Tomas over to Bollinsky. Maybe in a federal prison the rat couldn't get out. The jail in Nogales was a joke. Lucinda's money might bribe Tomas out to save him from testifying that she paid him to kidnap Maria. No matter the outcome, Slocum still needed to rescue the Teller girl from the old man before they left Harlequin and take her to Millie's.

"I can take him wherever you want," Baca said.

"I'll get the other girl and take her to Nogales. Meet you at the ranch in two days. Baca?" The youth looked up from the last of his food and rested the tortilla in his fingers. "Don't take any chances. Tomas tries anything, kill him."

"I savvy."

A half hour later, Slocum dismounted in front of the store. A Mexican mockingbird let out a tirade of whistles from a nearby limb. He wrapped the reins on the hitch rack, felt for the Colt, and satisfied it was free, mounted the steps. The bell rang overhead and the old man looked up.

"Need more matches, greaser?" Teller asked from his chair.

"No, I came for Lacey."

Teller's face blanched under his black beard and his red tongue showed in contrast when his jaw sagged. He started out of the chair, but stopped at the sight of Slocum's cocked gun.

"Imogene told me all about you. She's got enough to hang you, mister. Lacey, come out here."

"What are you saying?"

"I'm saying that you've been living in incest with your own daughters."

"Why! Why! That's a damn lie if she told you that."

"No, it ain't a lie, Paw." Lacey slipped into the room and edged her way behind the counter to keep a distance from him.

"Shut your mouth, girl!"

"I aim to blow daylight through your rotten guts if you move one more inch towards her," Slocum warned, satisfied by her words that what he had suspected was the truth.

"Lacey, I'll burn your ass. Now tell the man the truth, that it's all a lie!"

"No, no, not a lie. You hurt me bad." Tears began to run down her cheeks, and she shook her head at the man. "You know what you done!"

"Listen, this is all a family misunderstanding. She's just upset. She don't mean that, do you?" Teller bolted out of the chair.

Slocum shot a hole in the floor at the man's foot. "I won't shoot the floor next time. Get back in that chair." The billowing gun smoke smarted Slocum's eyes. If the man advanced on her again, he aimed to kill him.

Shaken, Teller half raised his hands and backed to the chair. Lacey darted past him and into the living quarters. Slocum turned to see the blacksmith burst in the door.

"What the hell is the shooting about?"

"Ease down," Slocum said to the smithy.

"That damn Messikin's robbing me! He's robbing me!"

In two steps, Slocum clubbed Teller over the head with the butt of his Colt and silenced him.

"No, Ruben!" Lacey cried, and rushed across the room to stop the big man before he stormed Slocum.

"What in hell's going on in here?" Ruben demanded, trying to get past the girl.

"I came to take Lacey to her sister in Nogales. This old man has been raping her."

"Raping her!" Ruben shouted.

"Easy," Slocum said.

"You never told me—" The man's great hand clasped her thin shoulders in his fingers and looked in her face. "Lacey, I didn't know—" Then he hugged her to his great chest.

"I couldn't tell you," she sobbed.

"Will you take Lacey to her sister in Nogales?" Slocum asked with an eye on Teller, who moaned on his hands and knees from the floor.

"No, I'll marry her."

"You don't have to," Lacey sniffled.

"We're going to be married. What about him?" Ruben asked Slocum.

"I'd say tie a tin can on his tail and send him back to Texas where he came from."

"I'll do that too," Ruben said with a grim nod. "He deserves worse, but I'll send him packing."

"Good. I've got to see about a prisoner."

"Who's that?"

"Tomas Morez. He's wanted for a kidnapping in Mexico."

"I'll be damned. You had me fooled. What's your name?"

"Slocum."

"Boy, Slocum, you sure turned Harlequin upside down this morning." He tucked Lacey under his arm with pride. "Get up and pack, you old buzzard. You're leaving here in ten minutes."

"But—" Teller struggled to his feet.

"You better be on your way in ten minutes or I'm kicking your butt to the New Mexico line," Ruben told him.

Slocum holstered his Colt and waved to the couple. Outside, he mounted the roan and looked hard at the weathered storefront, grateful for the smithy handling matters there, then turned his pony south. He planned to catch Baca and his prisoner in an hour.

17

Bollinsky stalked back and forth across the great hall with his hands clasped behind his back. His pristine uniform was creased and clean, his boots polished. A man deep in his own thoughts, he blinked as if shocked at the sight of Slocum coming through the front door.

"Maria said you went—"

"Baca and I went after Tomas Morez. We have him outside on a horse."

"Alive?"

"Yes, but we gave his money away so he couldn't bribe the jailers."

"I never thought of that. But my men usually split the money they find on such outlaws anyway."

"Slocum!" Maria rushed into the room and hugged him as if they were alone. Then she looked around for Bollinsky. "There you are—have you two talked?" she asked.

"We have," Slocum said. "Baca and I brought Tomas back. He doesn't know a thing about El Lobo or Montrose. The woman Lucinda hired him to kidnap you so you could not testify against her. He says she wanted him to kill you, but he said he couldn't kill a woman. He claims he hit me over the head and the dead man at her place named Gerald killed the guard."

"My, what a conscience. Kidnap, kill, what difference does it make? Both are serious crimes," Bollinsky said with a scowl of disapproval.

"Difference to Tomas anyway."

"I wish to go out there and horsewhip that little bastard," she said through her teeth.

"When?" Slocum asked, and poured himself some red wine in a pottery cup. It satisfied a portion of his thirst.

She shook her head and clutched her arms tightly. "I trusted him. That he would ride back here and tell my father of my plight. Instead he told that witch Lucinda that I was Don Obregon's daughter." She stared across the room, then shook her head in disbelief. "He came here and kidnapped me for her. Yes, he is worse than a killer."

"Let the law handle him." Slocum watched her inhale deeply. "You can never extract enough pain or torture from such a rotten piece of dung. It would only reduce you to his level."

She nodded, but did not turn back.

"I'm going to find the kitchen help," Slocum said, making a show of looking around. "Where is your help? Hiding? Two men are starving in your house and they're doing nothing about it. Nor is their boss."

"Oh, I will find you two some food. Both of you have a seat and some wine. You both are like growling dogs today."

"We're hungry, starving, that's why," Slocum said, and both men broke into laughter. She made a face at them from the doorway and disappeared.

Bollinsky filled himself a cup of wine and refilled Slocum's. "Here's to better days." He toasted with his mug.

"Much better ones," Slocum agreed.

After the large meal, the three of them retired to the tall chairs in the corner. Slocum felt mellow from the wine, and settled back in the comfort of the cushions.

"I must ride into the Sierras to once and for all run down this El Lobo," Bollinsky said.

"I have a better idea. What if a gringo hunter went in there with an Apache guide and his packer, say, to hunt for jaguars. Hired some local people to put up his tent, to sell him hay and grain for his horses, maybe hired a woman or two as camp cooks. He would need to be someone that El Lobo doesn't know on sight."

"It would be very dangerous. He would try to rob you if he thought you had any money." Bollinsky gave a concerned look at Slocum.

"But it might lure him out of hiding."

"That sounds far too dangerous to even think about," Maria protested. "The man is a cold-blooded killer."

"But his original gang is dead. He probably has some boys now for helpers. A few bronco Indians. How dangerous could they be?"

"Boys could kill you too."

"They can't be as tough as the ones that were executed." He turned to the captain for his opinion.

"No, but he is still—I don't know. It might work better than anything else."

"What I think too. Your Apache scout Raphael and I can go up there and try it."

"I will go as your camp cook," she said.

"He knows you." Slocum gave her a peeved look of disapproval. All he needed was to have to worry about her safety in those mountains.

"He knows Maria Cardinale Obregon, a frightened little girl in an expensive dress, not Lupe Ramaras."

"Too dangerous." Slocum was determined. She was not going up there with them, no matter how much she pleaded.

"I am the only one who knows him on sight."

"She has a point," Bollinsky said, and refilled their cups with more wine.

"Not much of one, but a point," Slocum said, still filled with misgivings.

"I will cut my hair short, and in the morning I will have it lightened on top. He won't know me."

Slocum closed his eyes. With her beautiful curls cut away and the top thatch turned a yellowish red, like some *putas* wore theirs, chances were good that El Lobo would not recall her in such a disguise. But Slocum did not think much of her getting involved in it—too risky. He needed to figure a way to dissuade her from going along. What could he do?

The rooster crowed a day later in the early morning, and Lupe Ramaras rushed about the yard shouting orders. The kitchen help packed beans and rice in the packs. "More weight in the panniers than the mules can carry," Baca said to Slocum.

Slocum watched her charging around; she definitely looked the role. The short-cut reddish-golden hair on top of her head tossed and glowed in the early morning light. Damn, he hated her cutting away her long curls.

With the red-rose pattern on a black pleated skirt in one hand, she waved and shouted at the poor help hustling about to fill her orders. The black blouse showed too much of her breasts, and even threatened to expose her nipples when she ran back to the house for something else.

At last, she hugged her house women one at a time, and waved at the grim-looking Franco, who oversaw everything like a disapproving father. In a bound, she was astride her mousy dun, and they rode out for the Sierra Madres. Slocum looked them over. His ragtag army, Baca and the Apache tracker Raphael at the head. Baca led the pack string of mules, and at the back of the train, Maria whipped the slower mules with a long quirt looped around her wrist. Slocum rode a single-footed tall sorrel behind her. He wore a suit, and his pants were tucked in knee-high polished boots she'd found for him to wear as part of his costume. With the pith helmet on his head, he felt certain he looked like some Eastern dude with money to burn in search of a trophy.

He glanced up at the round brim of his helmet and chuckled. They might mistake him for General George Crook, who never went outside without his headgear. The thing on his head would never replace a good felt hat, but it did add authenticity to his role.

The second day, they reached the foothills and entered the narrow winding canyon that led to the mountains. Slocum rode at the rear of the train as he spoke to Maria about the outlaw.

"This man Lobo. What does he look like?" he asked, moving to ride beside her where the canyon floor was wide enough for the both of them.

"He is tall for a *mexicano*. Has swarthy skin with even white teeth. His nose has a scar across it and his eyes are dark. Almost black. Oh, and a bushy mustache over his upper lip."

"Why do they call him Lobo?"

She shook her head. "He may have started that himself. He is a braggart and I don't think he is very smart."

"He's escaped Bollinsky before."

"So?"

"Bollinsky's a good soldier. I was with him. You know, I think the captain would like to court you."

She twisted around in the saddle and frowned at Slocum. "Did he say so?"

"No, but he hinted about it."

"You trying to tell me that you will soon leave me?"

"I'll have to."

"Oh, Slocum," she sighed, and shook her head in disapproval. "Won't you ever come back?"

"Don't make any plans about me."

Silence ruled their ride. The sharp ring of shod hooves on the exposed rock underlay in the canyon rang out. Mules brayed, snorted, and moved in single file. Maria avoided looking back at him. He knew she was upset, but they needed to face the facts. He couldn't stay there or any place for long.

"What if those bounty hunters never come?" She twisted in the saddle to look back at him.

"I'm sorry, Maria, they will come."

"I'll kill them," she said under her breath, but he heard her and smiled at her defiance.

He looked up at the towering walls that hemmed them in. The shade of mid-morning held the temperatures down. They still must mount the steep narrow trail. Maybe the dangers of the trail would occupy her mind. He turned and looked back at the twists that closed off his view of the valley behind them. Tonight they would sleep under blankets in the cooler heights.

Their climb up the narrow trail proved uneventful. When the sun formed a great red ball in the west, the wall tents were pitched to make their camp look authentic. A canvas fly was strung on ropes from jack pines to provide her with a kitchen under a shade. To the last detail, the camp resembled that of a rich man's expedition down to the canvas folding chair with arms that Slocum resided in. Baca and Raphael did the work in case they were being observed.

She crossed to where he sat and poured him a drink of rye in a glass. Then, squinting against the sun's glare, hand on her hip, she gave a sigh.

"You're working too hard," Slocum said.

"I'm living up to my part of the deal."

"Yes, but—"

"No. That bastard killed my father and sold me to Lucinda. I want him arrested and to pay for his crimes."

"Still—"

"Slocum, I could ride with you to hell and back."

"That is not the way I travel, and besides, what about the hacienda and the people that depend on you?"

She put her hands on her hips and shoved her small firm breasts forward. Then she gave him a hard look of disapproval, before she headed back to her cooking. He smiled at the swing and sway of her skirt, thinking about the shapely rock-hard butt under the cloth. Later.

In the darkness of twilight, the men squatted near the red coals in the rock circle, plates in their hands, and talked about the best places to set up the next camp. They planned to reach the Rio Blanco in two days and make it their permanent hunting camp.

"Sorry I can't help you," Slocum said, leaning forward in his chair for her to heap more rice and beans on his plate. The cooler air made him ravenously hungry.

"All this will fool them," Raphael said, and smiled.

"Yes," Baca agreed. "You look like a rich man who once came to hunt with the don."

"Just so the mountain people think so. We need to hire a few of them to help make camp, and to bring us cooking wood."

Baca and the Apache agreed with a nod, busy refilling their plates. Soon they would find some others to fill those roles. Money talked in an isolated society that was short on real coins and ways to earn them.

"You aren't a half-bad cook, Lupe," Slocum said, and the other two men laughed guardedly at his words.

She gave him a frown from her place seated on a log, but he saw the smile in the edge of her full lips. No doubt she really wanted this worthless outlaw apprehended and sent away. They both did. Mexican courts had no death sentence, but a lifetime in prison would be enough. It would stop Lobo's murdering and raiding.

In his tent later, Slocum made her undress and lay face-down on the cot. The orange flames of the candle lamp flickered on the bed stand and cast his shadow on the canvas wall and roof. Then he climbed up and straddled her legs. For a long moment he studied the shaded form under him. He drew a deep breath, then bent over her to begin working on her. His hands and fingers began to knead her shoulders. She turned her cheek to the side and gave moans of relief, while the balls of his thumbs sought the taut muscles and loosened them. He worked her silky skin down her supple spine. At last he massaged the span across her hips, and she cried out, then from relief collapsed in a pile.

"Oh, that felt so good," she muttered.

"Good." He rose, stepped off, and smiled down at her. With one boot toe he worked off the other boot, then sat on the opposite cot and pulled the second boot off. A rush of air filled the second boot when his foot eased out of it.

She rolled over, propped her head up with an elbow, and through half-opened eyes looked at him. "I like this Lupe business."

He stood up and undid his belt. "You haven't seen it all yet."

"Good. May I blow out the candle?" she asked.

"Sure," he said, stripping off his britches and looking at her luscious breasts. Filled with a strong need for her, he finished undressing and slipped beside her on the narrow cot, and their lips met. He closed his eyes and his mind to all of his concerns about the outlaw El Lobo.

The next day they packed up and were moving early. At mid-morning at the head of the train, Baca met a wood cutter on the trail. He was an older man with a bushy white beard who held his sombrero in front of him and nodded his head enthusiastically. From the rear at some distance, Slocum decided from his observations that they would have several suppliers hired before the day was out.

That afternoon, they camped by a small stream that yielded several small trout to Slocum's fishing. When gutted and cleaned, they made a feast thanks to Lupe's cooking. The wood cutter delivered a burro load of cooking sticks. Lupe took charge, talking loudly and telling the man they would need much more at the base camp they planned to set up on the Rio Blanco the next day.

"Oh, sí, Señora. I bring much wood to you there."

"Not all sticks, the gringo wants logs."

"Sí, bring you big logs. Cost more, though."

"How much more?" Hands on her shapely hips, she glared at the man.

"Dime more."

"Dime! That is robbery! Do I look stupid?"

"No, no, Señora."

"You bring me two loads of big logs and if they are good enough, I will pay your price, but I must satisfy that gringo over there. Do you savvy?"

"Savvy. I am pleased to bring you wood."

"Where is this woman does the washing?"

"Oh, she will be at the river tomorrow."

"Fine. Is there someone who I can hire to help me cook?"

"Yes, my sister."

"Is she very clean?"

"Oh, yes."

"Send her along." Then Lupe shook her head as if the matter was all too much. Seated in his chair, Slocum forced back a grin, crossed his legs, and went back to reading the thick book on mining from her father's library.

When the little man and his burros plodded off, she brought him a cup of steaming coffee.

"Well, we will have enough people hired at the next camp." She put her hands on her hips and stretched her back. "And I'll be ready by dark for another back rub."

He laughed, and then agreed he would do it. Through the vapors from his coffee, he studied the pine-clad slopes. Over the next craggy range, they would drop into the drainage of the Blanco. No telling how many days it would take to spring their trap. Still, things continued to work according to his plan. He sat back and considered the matter—they were drawing closer to building the snare for Lobo.

At mid-afternoon, they dropped over the top, and Slocum could see the sparkling ribbon far below. Like a string of diamonds, the river shone bright under the high sun, with pale green cottonwoods lining the shores. He booted the sorrel down the slope and unlimbered the fancy Remington shooting rifle. Somewhere between them and the water, they would jump a fat mule deer out of the manzanita and mountain mahogany.

The sorrel headed off the sandy slope on his hind quarters, and slid to the bench below. Slocum sent him down a dim game trail while searching for the sight of a gray head. Then, to his right, a rack stuck out of the brush and the buck flicked his ears at the intruder. Slocum sighted down the telescopic sight and found a place behind the buck's front legs in the gray-black hide. The rifle's report carried in waves across the valley and then back again in echoes. The buck jumped, went twenty yards, then tumbled end over end.

Raphael rode past him. "Good shot."

"Can you handle it?" Slocum asked under his breath.

"Sí, patrón." The Apache winked at him knowingly and sent his bay off the mountain after the carcass.

Two new brush-covered ramadas waited for them on the riverbanks. They were obviously new, for the leaves on the limbs were not even wilted. Several smiling women stood about with their dark-eyed, naked children hiding behind their skirts.

Lupe dismounted and began taking charge. "Baca, set the *señor*'s chair under that shade over there. This one is for my cooking."

"Who is the washerwoman?" she asked, looking the women over.

"I am." The buxom woman stepped forward. "My name is Thelam."

"Good, Thelam," Lupe said to her. "I have much for you to do tomorrow. But I will pay you for coming today. Who is the cook?"

"I am. My name is Sena."

"Good, we have a deer to dress before we can cook supper. Pick some help from the others and we'll get started."

Slocum went off to where the men were unloading the mules. Three young men helped them, taking Baca's orders on what to do. Slocum stood aside and observed.

The wood cutter's burros brayed coming off the mountain, and he soon arrived with the wood. He and Lupe argued about price, and in the end she paid him his money.

Tents soon stood in place. The mules and horses were watered and taken to graze downstream by two of the younger boys. Things bustled around the camp. Baca did the bossing and the new workers, eager to please, soon had things arranged to suit him.

Raphael rode off on his horse to scout game for Slocum to hunt. A logical enough reason, Slocum decided, and sat back in his chair. Overhead the rustle of the cottonwood leaves and the songs of the many birds made a lullaby for him to listen to while he thought about his next move. It depended on what Raphael found or didn't find on his search.

Somewhere out there, perhaps even observing them, the

killer-kidnapper was waiting. Slocum took off his pith helmet and sat back. The afternoon breeze lightly lifted his hair and cooled him. If his plan didn't work, Bollinsky could storm the mountains again, but somehow Slocum felt his scheme would produce the outlaw.

Besides, since he'd mentioned leaving her, he could hardly satisfy Maria with enough action each night in bed. Maybe a witch had turned her into Lupe; he smiled to himself at the notion. He closed his eyes and savored his recall of the heady moments they shared each evening.

The next day, he and the Apache rode into the mountain peaks. At midday, the Apache, who had found no sign of the outlaw the day before, discovered the spore of a huge mountain lion. He signaled for Slocum to join him.

"This is a big cat."

"Good. The bigger he is, the more they will believe I am only a hunter."

Raphael nodded, swung in the saddle, and waved for Slocum to follow. Slocum sent the sorrel after him, and they climbed the steep game trail winding through the trunks of pines. At last, they dismounted and Slocum drew his single-shot target rifle from the scabbard. The Apache dropped to his knee to search the dust. Finally he nodded that he had found sign, and they hurried over the giant boulders and between them.

Then Raphael threw out his hand to stop Slocum. He motioned with his head that the cat was somewhere above them. Slocum wondered how he knew where the cat was at, but he respected the man's skill at tracking. Then, from the rocks twenty feet above their heads, came the cry of a large cat.

Slocum pressed his shoulder to the granite surface, sighted through the scope, and when the cat's face appeared and looked over the edge, Slocum's heart stopped. With the tawny-colored chest locked in his sights, the rifle gave a sharp report in the close confines. Then the lion tumbled off the ledge and dropped with a thud at their feet. Slocum caught up on his breathing and slowly brought the rifle down. Big cat. They had the trophy they needed.

"*Mucho* big one," Raphael said, impressed, when he poked it with a stick to be certain it was dead. The cat never moved.

"Make a bully good mount," Slocum said, and then laughed. "Bully good."

The camp help came out to see the hide slung over Raphael's lap when they rode into camp. Women and men both exclaimed over it as if they thought the lion was a really great trophy too.

Later, Slocum and Baca were alone under the ramada.

"Any word on the outlaw?"

"Yes. They said he took a girl against her will from a village nearby, and the people here are very angry about it."

"Would they show the way to his camp?"

"They don't know where he hides now, or I think they would go and try to get the girl back. She was the village chief's daughter and a favorite one. She scorned Lobo's offer to marry him and so he took her against her will."

Slocum drew on his fresh cigar. There had to be a way to find him. He blew the smoke slowly out his lips and considered the matter. So close and yet so far—there had to be a way.

"If they are that mad at him, perhaps you could tell them you think the gringo hunter might hunt for him."

"Someone may not be mad at Lobo and would warn him. He cannot stay in these mountains without some help, so he has friends and I fear they're in the camp too."

"Good thinking," Slocum agreed. He drew on the cigar again. Patience. He needed lots of it. He blew out the smoke. *El Lobo, your days are numbered anyway.*

18

Outside the tent, Slocum vented his bladder. The cool predawn breeze swept his face while he studied the star-lighted camp and finished the pressing task that had awakened him from the warm nest that he shared with Maria's smooth body. Through at last, he shoved it inside his pants and rebuttoned his fly. Where was the outlaw? Someone had to know where he was hiding.

A mule in his sleep snorted on the picket line over the hiss of the river. Another stomped his hoof in a dream. Slocum tried to see under the ramadas. Nothing moved, yet he wondered why he felt so apprehensive. Vulnerability was probably what made him itch. No sign of anyone or anything, only the ancient gnarled cottonwood leaves rustling overhead. Yet something was afoot. He slipped back in the tent, eased his six-shooter out of the holster. Redwood pistol grip in his fist, he came outside like a ghost. Then he made his way slowly through the camp. The wooden arms and the white canvas of his chair were visible in the dim light.

Keeping his back toward the river where nothing showed but the sparkling rushing water, he edged his way toward the makeshift kitchen shelter. He glanced skyward at a thousand stars through the twisting leaves. His bare soles moved over the loose sandy ground, finding an occasional twig or sharp object to jab them.

The two men were asleep in their bedrolls beyond the last traces of red coals in the fire pit. Something made him look up and in an instant, he saw a large blur from the limb flying at him. He fired twice before the weight of the large cat struck him flat on the ground.

Out of wind, he struggled to escape the dying lion's hind feet scratching in the throes of death. With the rank animal smell strong in his nose, and spitting a mouthful of cat hair, he wiggled out from beneath it. On hands and knees at last, he huffed for air. Satisfied the cat would soon die, he stood up.

"Señor?" Baca shouted, and rushed from his bedroll. "You all right?"

"Fine—now."

"Mother of God—" Both Baca and Raphael looked at the dark, still creature on the ground.

Baca struck a match and bent over the cat. "It is the mate of the other one, ain't it?"

"Could be. How did you know it was here?" Raphael asked Slocum.

"I don't know. Something wasn't right. I came down to check on you two."

"Slocum? Slocum?" Lupe cried, and came running wrapped in a blanket. "What's happened here?"

"A lion came looking for his mate." He pointed his Colt at the dead lion.

"Oh, my God, you could have been killed."

Others came running up the sandy beach from their makeshift hovels. Their nervous low voices could be heard as they drew closer.

Baca went for a lamp, and Raphael examined the cat in the dark.

"You shot it once in the head and once under the front

leg," the Apache said. He rose to his feet as Baca returned and held the orange light over the tawny furred invader. The others peeked at it. One small brave boy edged his way up close enough and jabbed the cat with a stick, then flew back for fear it was still alive. His moves drew nervous laughter from the others.

"I was just lucky." Slocum hugged the upset Lupe under his arm. She trembled, and he wished to settle her concerns. It was over for him. *Close* was a part of his life. It was the ones that got you that were bad.

"Maybe we should move our camp?" she asked, sounding worried.

"And miss all this good hunting?" he said for everyone's ears. "Why, no. We're staying right here."

"How did you know it was up there?" Baca finally asked.

"Pure luck. I saw it move at the last minute and had the Colt in my hand."

Baca nodded, but in the light, Slocum could see the young man was still in disbelief.

"I must go dress," Lupe said to excuse herself. "Time for me to start fixing breakfast."

"Yes, it is time," Slocum said, and released her.

Raphael hung the cat off a limb to skin it.

"It can wait until daylight," Slocum told them.

The two men agreed, and the others tested the fur with the backs of their hands. Obviously the handful of mountain people were in awe of another dead cat. Good, it made his presence even more believable.

Slocum didn't go hunting in the morning. Raphael removed the pelt and went looking for more sign of big game. Slocum cleaned the fancy sporting rifle. That and the Colt were purged and re-oiled. In mid-afternoon, he left the camp with a towel to find a deep pool to soak in. He waved to Lupe, obviously busy with her help making the next meal. She nodded in approval. Upstream, where the willow and brush grew higher, would afford him some privacy from the women's eyes and all the children that shrieked about the camp.

He undressed, then hung his clothing and holster on some limber branches. Gingerly, on his bare soles, he crossed the gravel bar until the water quickly came to his knees. Then he dove into the chilly rush. It felt good to swim under the surface, and at last he came up, scraping away the water from his face and hair with his hands.

He didn't hear the words behind him clear enough, but he swiveled on his feet.

"Where's your money, gringo?"

No mistaking the identity of the big man who stepped down from a too-small mountain pony. The deep scar over the bridge of his nose accented his dark hate-filled eyes. His black beard was matted and untrimmed, and he looked the part of the outlaw Slocum had expected.

"Don't shoot, mister. I can pay you," Slocum said, and started to wade to the bank. "I have—plenty money—" He hoped he looked afraid enough, coming out of the river with his hands held high.

"Move along, gringo." Lobo waved the barrel of his revolver to hurry him.

"Can I put on my pants?" Slocum asked.

"Yeah, wouldn't want some of those women to see that big dick anyway." Lobo laughed at his own joke and, satisfied the pants had no weapons in them, tossed them to him.

Slocum dressed quickly. Where was Baca? He didn't need the boy getting shot up.

"How much money you got in camp?"

"Hundreds—more than that. It's in my chest. I'll show you. Don't shoot me."

"Get to hiking." Sounding impatient, Lobo waved his

pistol for Slocum to head to the camp. "I can use a good stake."

"I can pay you, mister," Slocum said, wincing on whatever stabbed his sole.

"What's your name?"

"John Gadberry, Mobile, Alabama."

"Big-game hunter, huh?"

"I don't mean you any harm. You can have my trophies." Slocum raised his voice, hoping the ones in camp would hear them coming. Women and children didn't need to be hurt. Nor did Maria. He had to hope that Lobo didn't recognize her.

He could see the camp ahead. The others fell back at the sight of him coming with his hands in the air. Women protectively took their children to their skirts, watching with horror on their faces as the two men went by.

"Don't try anything," Lobo warned, pointing his pistol at them. "I only came for his money."

Slocum wondered if with the distraction of all the camp workers, he might have a chance to reach the man. If he could ever wrestle the man's gun hand away—no, he might get one of them wounded or killed by a stray bullet.

"Which tent is yours?" Lobo demanded.

"Second one," Slocum said, and stopped before the tent flap.

"Let me see in there," Lobo said, looking all around to be certain there wasn't another threat to him. He lifted the flap with his free hand and gave a peek inside. "Where's it at?"

"In the big locked trunk."

"Get in there and don't try anything."

"Sure," Slocum said, and kicked the man hard in the crotch. He knew he hit part of his goal when Lobo bent forward in a deep gasp. Slocum slammed the wrist of Lobo's gun hand against the tent pole, splintering the post with the force, and the revolver flew away. Slocum took a hard fist to the right cheek from Lobo, and gave back an uppercut that clicked the outlaw's teeth together.

Shaken by the facial blow, Slocum's right eye flickered, and he realized it would soon be swollen shut. He tried to find footing under his bare soles in the soft sand. Lobo drew a hunting knife from behind him. The blade gleamed in the sunlight, and he swished it past Slocum's bare stomach.

"You sumbitch, I'll gut you!" Lobo screamed at him.

Slocum searched about for a stick; anything to defend himself with. Moving back each time from the man's slashing attack, he tried to think of anything he could use. Lobo struck at him again and again, trying to close in with each thrust.

Then Slocum noticed the flap part on the second tent. He feinted away from the blade again, and barely missed the tip's honed point. Saliva ran from the corners of Lobo's mouth, his face fiery red with rage.

"All I wanted was your damn money! Now I'll cut your balls out before I get through with you!"

The Remington's muzzle stuck out the tent flap and it blasted smoke out the muzzle with the round. Struck in the chest by the bullet, Lobo staggered sideways, groaned like a dying hog, and began to teeter on his feet.

"You've killed me," he cried, going to his knees. The knife flew from his hand, and Slocum swept it away.

Lobo blinked his eyes in disbelief at the tent and the woman who emerged with the smoking rifle in her hands. He coughed deep, then with pained effort tried to look up at her.

"Do you know me now?" Maria demanded.

"No—" he gasped, holding his chest with his hand where the blood rushed out of him. "Who—the—hell—are—you?"

"Maria Cardinale Obregon."

19

Raphael returned before they finished burying Lobo. He nodded solemnly at what he saw, and dismounted his horse near the prone corpse on the ground.

"I knew he was coming, so I hurried back. Sorry I am so late." The Apache squatted down on his haunches. "He killed a pretty girl back there. Her body is in a cave." He motioned toward the peaks with a toss of his head.

Waist-deep in the grave with the spade in his hands, Baca looked up at Slocum. "What should we do about her?"

"I will go tell the women from the camp," Slocum said, and rose to his feet. "They can send a party for her body. I am certain they will want to do that."

"It was not a good way for her to die," Raphael said after him.

Slocum nodded that he had heard the warning. He didn't need the gruesome details. He found the camp women huddled in the shade. Even the children still seemed stunned by the outlaw's appearance and his death.

"Raphael has found a girl in a cave that Lobo killed. Someone should go for her body."

His words drew shrieks of crying from the already upset women. The washerwoman rose and went back with him to learn the location of the body. She stood stone-faced and grim and listened to Raphael's directions to the cave. Obviously she knew the place he spoke about. She thanked him very quietly, then went back to the others.

Lobo was buried without word or ceremony, except that Baca and Raphael crossed themselves when they finished covering him up. The three went back to the camp and in silence began to pack the mules. Maria had the panniers loaded, save for the extra food she had given earlier to the camp women.

"I paid the helpers well," she said.

Slocum nodded in agreement, and went to help the men load the mules. That night they camped under the stars on the western slopes of the mountains and slept in their bedrolls without tents.

"Hold me close," Maria whispered, crawling in his blankets. "I need to be held all night long."

"I understand," he said, and curled around her. Somewhere off in the night, a wolf howled mournfully and Slocum agreed with him. *It is an empty world when you are alone.*

The next day at noon, they reached the brink of the canyon. Slocum checked her cinch to be certain it was tight, and slapped down the stirrup.

"Why do I feel this may be our last day together?" she asked.

"Because women are witches and they know things before they happen."

"Did you know that I knew you were coming to Montrose's camp before you ever arrived there. I knew in my heart that someone was coming to help me. I didn't realize it then, but I knew, had the feeling like I have now."

"We better mount up and get off this mountain."

"I don't dread the ride down—" He forced her to mount up, then clapped her on the leg.

"It'll be all right," he said to reassure her.

They reached the bottom two hours later, and spilled out of the canyon onto the desert floor at sundown.

"There will be a moon and we can ride by it to the hacienda," Baca said.

"Let's ride on then," she said.

Slocum agreed, and they crossed the desert under the bold moonlight. By midnight the crescent hung low in the southwest sky, and the outline of the distant main house glowed like a large pearl in the night.

"I'm glad to be back," she said.

"You enjoyed being Lupe," he teased her.

"I would be Lupe in the morning and ride on without a complaint if you would take me with you."

"I can't, Lupe," he said, and looked across the dark rows of grapes they rode past after speaking to the guard. "No way."

"I won't ever forget you."

"You better," he said under his breath.

"When will you leave me?"

A lump rose in his throat and he shook his head without an answer. But he felt as she did, that his time spent with her was fast coming to an end. He didn't like the crawly feeling on the back of his neck warning him he needed to ride on, nor the gut-wrenching that tore at him over leaving her.

The next morning, half asleep and trying to wake himself up, so he could leave before she awoke, Slocum stumbled into the great room. He blinked at the sight of Franco seated at the great table drinking coffee and obviously waiting for him. Slocum's eyes burned and would hardly focus on the man. Fogged by a lack of enough sleep and the long haul they'd made to return, his brain acted sluggish. But he knew the man was there for a reason.

"Morning, amigo," Slocum said.

"Morning."

"You have something for me?"

"*Sí.* First, there is word for you that two men are in Nogales asking about you."

"Are they the Abbott brothers?"

"*Sí.*"

"What else?" Damn, he'd known they couldn't be far behind. Wondering about his next move, he raked his fingers through his uncombed hair. That would make his departure even swifter.

"This man Montrose you asked me to check on. He has vanished. Since they broke out of jail, no one knows where he or any of his men have gone."

"I have a good idea where they are at. Thanks. These men in Nogales—any more word on them or where they are at?"

"No, Señor. But it has been a few days since I received the news about them."

"So they could be headed this way?"

"They won't ever take you on this hacienda." Franco's frown caused his bushy eyebrows to form a straight line.

Slocum nodded to show he understood the man's intentions. Still, he could not involve innocent people in his own troubles. He'd better ride on and shortly. He looked up and smiled at the kitchen girl who brought him a steaming mug of coffee. Time for him to vamoose.

With the horse wrangler pointing out various animals, Slocum picked a tough mustang from the remuda, a yellowish brindle-striped gelding with half of his left ear cut off either by accident or on purpose. Many times while "earing" down a bronc for a rider to get on it, with half of the ear clamped in the cowboy's teeth and a head lock around the pony's neck to hold him down for the rider, in the excitement the ear was bitten off. The gelding looked sound enough, and double tough despite his runty stature. But it didn't take a big horse to carry a man a long ways. It took a stout one. An animal that could easily live off the land. When his rider stopped, he dropped his head and went to gathering forage. And also one who didn't need grain to sustain his strength.

After the *vaquero* roped the pony for him and nodded his approval at Slocum's choice, he took the lead and led the snorty horse from the corral to the blacksmith. He asked the smithy to shoe him. The man smiled, and told him he would have him ready in no time. Slocum glanced toward the house. It would have been better if he had ridden out earlier instead of taking so much time.

"Señor?" When Slocum turned, he saw Baca hurrying across the yard.

Slocum waited for the young man.

"Are you leaving?" Baca asked.

Slocum nodded. "What is it?"

"I would like to ride along with you."

"Better not. My trail needs to be dim and it isn't fun."

"I would like you to show me those things."

"Find a good woman, marry her, have a family. It is a better life than mine."

"And become an old man?"

"Ain't too exciting, but it sure beats eating tough jerky and drinking gyp water on some windswept mountain and not knowing where your next meal's coming from."

"I would like to try it."

Slocum considered the notion. He rubbed his palm over his mouth and felt the sharp edge of his uncut whiskers. Hell, the boy probably wouldn't stay hooked on this place anyway. Had to get so much out of his system anyway.

"Get a horse, bedroll. We'll ride a ways together. Can't promise you for how long."

"Oh, Señor!"

"No more oh, Señor. I'm Sloeum. You call me that and on the trail we're equal."

"I understand."

Slocum looked hard at the handsome boy, perhaps nineteen. Damn shame to drag him off, but there was nothing else to do but let him tag along. Might change his mind in a week or two. It damn sure wouldn't be as exciting as it had been riding with him chasing down Tomas and Lobo.

"I will be ready, Slocum."

"Better tell your folks you're going so they don't worry," he said after him, but he doubted the boy heard him.

Slocum raised his gaze to the house. Filled with dread, he knew that Maria would be up by this time. He would need to tell her about the bounty men and his plans. That would be tougher than the rest. Better get in there and take his bitter medicine.

When he entered the front door, she blinked her sleepy eyes at him and rose from her chair. "So you planned to leave without waking me?"

"I planned to leave." He took another steaming cup of coffee from the servant girl and looked at Maria.

"I've decided to go too," she said.

He closed his eyes and dropped his head. "You can't. There is no one to take care of this place. You have obligations here."

"Franco can handle it."

"No, he is not the owner. A ranch like this needs an owner."

"Slocum, please—let me go with you. I am not some spoiled rich girl. I can do my share," she pleaded.

"It isn't you. I know you're special, but dammit, this isn't the same thing. You know how tough it was up there in Montrose's camp. I live that way every day." He clenched his teeth and wished this argument had never happened. His fault. He should have ridden on by this time.

"Leave me then!" She began to cry, and ran from the room with her fists in her eyes.

He watched her retreat and turned on his heel. Time for him to go. He couldn't convince her of anything. Damn. He slammed on his hat and went outside. In the bright sun, he strode to the smithy.

"One more shoe." With the hoof in his lap, the man smiled while nailing on the left hind shoe.

Franco led up a mule loaded with supplies. Slocum could see the panniers were full.

"She would want you to have this."

"*Gracias,*" Slocum said, and accepted it. "She may only wish me in hell."

"She will understand someday. For all the people here, we are grateful you returned her to us. Her mother was very headstrong too."

Slocum acknowledged the man's words. When the farrier finished, he saddled the gelding. In the process of getting ready he decided to call the mustang Diablo. He'd been catching the devil from her. He might as well ride out on him.

Baca joined him, and they left the hacienda leading the mule. No sign of her. Slocum figured it was for the best. In time she would find someone for a husband. Perhaps the straight-backed captain. He wondered about Bollinsky. He would not get to tell the man that El Lobo was dead, but Bollinsky would learn on his next visit to the hacienda. Yes, they would make a good pair, spunky Maria and the always proper captain.

At the end of the vineyard he reined up, looked back at the main house. It rose like a fortress above the orchards and green fields. *Good-bye Maria.* He nodded to Baca and without a word, they short-loped their mounts off into the desert.

• • •

Slocum hurried up the steps to Millie's apartment. The grit on his boot soles ground into the wooden flights. He rapped on the thin door.

"She is at work. Go away," Imogene said from behind the peeling painted panels.

"Slocum. Open up."

"Who is with you?" she asked, peeking out the crack.

"A friend. I have word of your sister Lacey."

"What do you know about her?" she asked in hushed surprise, opening the door for him and Baca to enter. Dressed in a shapeless white cotton nightgown that swallowed her, she closed the door quickly behind them.

"She is marrying a blacksmith at Harlequin. He's a good man who will treat her well, and the man sent your father packing for Texas when he found out the truth about him."

"Lacey marrying? Why, she's still—"

"Old enough. He's a real man and I judge he'll protect her. She is out of the old man's hands." Then he remembered his traveling companion, who stood holding his hat. "This is Baca. He helped me get her away from him. I'd have brought her here, planned to, but the two of them were so set on getting married."

She nodded politely to Baca and hugged her arms to her chest as if she was cold. "Thanks for the news. I won't worry about her then."

"When will Millie be back?"

"In a few hours. You can wait in here or on the roof. Are you hungry?"

"We haven't eaten since morning."

"My, it must be close to midnight," she said, sounding concerned. "I have some cold—"

"That is good enough. We didn't come to disturb you. I only need to speak to her."

"Millie would want you fed." She waved them to the

doorway to the roof. "I will bring it out to you."

"Fine." He motioned for Baca to join him.

Once on the roof, each of them sat on a hammock and listened to the night sounds of bands playing music, the shouts and laughter of revelers, and the shrieks of *putas*.

"That is the sister?" Baca asked softly.

"Yes, nice girl."

"She is very pretty."

"Nice-looking," Slocum agreed, his mind not on her at the moment. He wanted to know where the Abbott Brothers went after Nogales. Since Millie knew them on sight and all about them, maybe she could tell him. Then he and the boy could hightail it in the other direction.

"She isn't married?" Baca asked.

"No." Then a smile crossed Slocum's lips when he realized the young man was stricken by Imogene. "Go help her. She needs some help, I'm certain."

"It would be—?"

"Yes, it's all right. Go ahead," he said, and had to suppress a laugh. He had forgotten about the first time a girl had turned his head. How tongue-tied he had become in her presence and how uncertain. Baca had it bad.

He rocked a little and watched the youth get up and go back downstairs. Soon he heard them talking. Good, Imogene spoke Spanish. Made it lots easier on the boy. He'd get all messed up figuring the right words to say in English.

In a short while she delivered Slocum a bottle of wine and said that his friend was nice.

"Good man," he agreed, and poured himself some in the goblet she gave him.

She hurried away, and the two of them must have conversed nonstop for the next few minutes. At last they brought out food for him, then went back inside as if he didn't exist. He took up a corn tortilla and smiled after them. The food smelled delicious and he began to eat. His state of hunger was sharp enough, anything would have helped it.

He had almost forgotten about them when he heard something crash. He looked up and frowned. Baca's face appeared in the lighted doorway.

"Is nothing—" And he disappeared.

Slocum shrugged off any concern. Finished with his food, he thought he heard some strained sounds coming from the apartment. He poured himself some more wine and sat back. He heard grunts and small groans from beyond the doorway, but tried not to pay any attention.

In a short while, Baca came outside and took his place on the opposite hammock. Even in the moonlight he looked pale. Then Imogene brought a second bottle of wine with her.

"Need some more?" she asked.

"No, I still have some," Slocum said, seeing the way she held her shoulders back and the look she gave Baca while offering the wine.

The youth rubbed his palms on top of his legs, then looked up and nodded at Imogene. "If you will have some with me."

"I won't tell a soul," Slocum said to dismiss her concern.

"Fine," she said, and sat down beside Baca. "Where is your cup?" she asked, looking around. Then she bounded off after one, and quickly returned with it.

Slocum felt like an intruder, but he didn't offer to move. Maybe he would nap. He swung his boots up and stretched out.

"Good night. Have Millie wake me up when she gets here." He rolled over on his side and closed his eyes. Sleep came fast. He was uncertain what made him wake up, but he stole a glance to the other swing and saw her bare legs in the air. On top of her, Baca was pounding away. Slocum shut his eyes and went back to sleep.

"Who's sleeping with her?" a voice hissed in his ear.

"Huh?"

"Dammit, Slocum, who is with her?" Millie demanded in a hoarse whisper.

"Shush, they've been having fun. Where you been?"

"I had a private poker game after work with a gentleman."

"My, my," he said.

"Wasn't what you think." Under the starlight, she gave another peevish look at the couple in the other bed.

"Dammit, you were young once. He's a good boy."

"You know them gawdamn Abbotts have been here?"

"That's why I came by," he whispered as she lay down with him.

"It wasn't to see me?"

"Hell, I'm here, ain't I?"

"They rode for Delores. Word was out you were down there."

"Good," he said, and blew in her ear.

She threw her hands up and made a face. "We can't do it with them over there."

"Why not. They did it with me over here."

"Oh, for gawd's sakes, Slocum, you always come at the most awkward times."

Then his lips silenced her and with his move, the hammock threatened to dump them out. Then both of them began to chuckle, until at last they spilled out on their butts. She glared at him in the starlight. "Jesus, you're a mess, Slocum."

He thought so too, leaned forward, and kissed her. The Abbotts were going south. Him and that horny boy could ride north at daybreak. If Baca was going along with him. Millie's perfume ran up and tickled his nose. Damn.

20

At dawn the two of them rode up the dusty road toward Tucson underneath the gnarled cottonwoods that tracked the shallow Santa Cruz River. They were three or four days from Bloody Basin. Slocum intended to go up there and put an end to Montrose's reign of terror. He felt certain the outlaw had returned to his canyon hideout. Once and for all Slocum intended to settle with the big man. The image of Montrose openly raping that rancher's wife still grated his conscience. The hell that outlaw had put Maria through, even killing the cattle—it all counted against him. Slocum only worried about the boy on the bay pony beside him. Was Baca up to such a test?

Montrose would damn sure test them.

"I'm going after that bunch of outlaws that bought their way out of prison," he said to Baca. Strange how he considered the nineteen-year-old a boy. At the same age he would have been furious to have been considered a boy, but he had no intention of demeaning the handsome youngster.

"You know where they are?" Baca asked, sounding taken aback.

"Where they were when I rescued Maria from them. They have a canyon to hide in."

"What will we do?"

"I don't know yet. Ain't got a good plan thought out. I simply wanted to warn you if it will do any good. Those outlaws are killers. We could be killed."

"I'll take my chances."

"That girl back there—"

"Someday I will ride back and see her." Baca grinned.

"There may not be a someday," Slocum said, and waited for his reply.

"Then I won't ride by. Slocum, I am riding with you."

"Sounds kind of exciting, don't it? Sleep with a pretty girl and next go shoot up some outlaws."

Baca pursed his lips together and nodded.

"Well, last night was as close as you get to heaven in this business, and from here on I can assure you it will all be hell."

"I won't disappoint you."

"I never doubted that. I'm saying right here, you can turn that horse around, go back, and marry that girl and never miss a thing."

A slow smile turned up the corners of his mouth. "I am riding with you."

"Well, you're a damn sight bigger fool than I thought." Halfway angry at himself and the boy, Slocum made Diablo short-lope.

In Tucson, Slocum bought dynamite, fuses, and caps. They carried the two wooden cases out of the store and prepared to load them. He turned to Baca.

"We better watch old Sly here. He takes a bucking fit, we sure need to duck and be certain he ain't around us."

"He could sure go bang, couldn't he?" Baca asked with his mischievous smile.

"Not while we're around, I hope," Slocum said, and they redid the canvas cover and the diamond hitch.

• • •

The second day they crossed the Salt and reached Ft. McDowell. Slocum knew a Yavapia who had scouted with him. They rode along the river until he found some young Indian women coming along, and he asked them about Benny Red Shirt.

Between their giggles, one of the girls, holding her hand over her mouth and taking strong appraising looks at Baca, explained that Red Shirt lived further upstream. They should look for a corral on the right, she directed in her broken English.

Slocum thanked them, and then with a grin asked, "Would you buy him from me?"

The girls ducked their heads and staggered about, laughing at his words. One or two still stole glances at the boy. He looked over at Baca, and could see the boy's face turning red.

"It was only an idea," he said to him, and spurred Diablo on. "Hell, you can't help that those women think you're handsome."

"I was not interested," Baca said when his horse caught up with Slocum's.

"Them Injun women get a lot prettier to look at. You haven't been in the mountains for a long enough spell yet."

Baca shook his head as if he would never change his mind.

"It's nice to be young and choosy," Slocum said, and drew Diablo down to trot.

They found Benny by the corral. He had two new horses inside the trap. Slocum could tell by their long tails that they were freshly captured. A big-headed man with a dark complexion, Benny wore an unblocked hat and a red shirt. His trademark. The Yavapia acted more interested in the mustangs than talking to them.

Slocum joined him and leaned on the top mesquite pole beside him. Indians had certain ways. When they were thinking, they did not like their thoughts mixed with other ideas. So Slocum waited for the man to decide to talk to him.

"That one horse has a watch eye," Benny said at long last.

"I saw that."

"They see things different than horse with brown ones."

"Oh?"

"It makes things much bigger with that glass eye like a telescope only close up bigger."

"That make them spookier than other horses?"

"Yes. I wish I had a boy to ride him."

"Getting too old to ride them?"

"Glass-eyed ones." Benny nodded firmly.

Slocum turned and looked for Baca. He saw the boy was already in the shade of a cottonwood and taking a siesta. He decided to let him sleep.

"Maybe when he wakes up, he will ride it?" Slocum indicated the slumbering Baca.

Benny nodded and turned back to the corral. "You didn't come here to see about him riding my crazy horse?"

"No. There's some outlaws up north in Bloody Basin. They've been raping squaws and white women as well as killing cattle."

"Bad hombres. They call that big one Montrose. Indians get plenty blame for those dead cattle too."

"Me and that boy are headed up there to see what we can do about him. You want to go along?"

"Can that boy ride my horse first?"

"I reckon so. Is it that important?"

"Pretty important. I caught him last Sunday off in the mountains. He came out of a blind canyon and I roped him. You know how I catch horse?"

"Yes, I have been with you when you did the same thing."

"Well, see, I have worried since then—should I have caught him or not?"

"How's that?"

"I don't know if he is a spirit horse or not and if I should turn him loose."

"I'll wake the boy up for such an important thing."

Slocum went to where Baca slept. "Hey, Benny's got a horse here that he needs ridden so we can go on."

Half asleep, Baca looked up at him and held his sombrero aside. "What kind of a horse?"

"Mustang he rounded up. You game to try him?"

"Sure." And he struggled to his feet. "That him in the corral?"

Slocum nodded and fell in behind him.

"He ever been rode?"

"Nope, you're the first. That make a difference?"

"Sure. Those sour ones can be hell to ride."

Slocum agreed, and Baca stripped the rig off his bay. Then, carrying it and the pads, he strode to the pen. He glanced over at the pair of horses.

"Which one?" he asked Benny.

"The sorrel."

"Figures. Got a watch eye, ain't he?" Baca dragged his rig through the gate. Then Slocum, with some effort, pulled it shut after him. "I need your riata," Baca said over his shoulder, and crowded the horses into the far side.

Slocum went for it, and turned to listen to Baca talk to the nervous colts. Obviously this was not the boy's first time in a wild-horse pen. Slocum brought back the lariat and stuck it over the fence for Baca.

"Let's get this other one out of the trap," Baca said without looking at Slocum and Benny. His attention was centered on the animals.

"He can go in that small one," Benny said, and ambled off to open the gap.

With the youth's hands to direct them, the horses bolted

past him and the opening. Baca acted unfussed, and
crowded them again. This time the bay split off and
ducked in the side pen.

His action upset the sorrel. He reared and screamed.
Benny gave the mustang a hard look, as if he was getting
apprehensive about the horse's ties to the supernatural.

Then the sorrel began to run around the pen in a good
open lope, thinking he could escape this threat to him if
he ran fast enough. The loop settled over his head, and
Baca jerked the slack tight so the horse's throat was captured. Then he set down on it, and the horse stopped with
some stiff leg hops.

Slocum expected him to wrap the rope around the snub-
bing post, but instead, Baca worked up the rope. The colt
struck at him with a forefoot, but quickly Baca dodged
the animal's efforts to protect himself that he'd learned as
a colt. Obviously this process would take some time, so
Slocum decided to unsaddle Diablo and the pack mule.

"Sure," Benny said when Slocum asked him about doing it. The former scout's attention was riveted on the
action in the corral.

Slocum looked up and noticed three of the young girls
from the road were sauntering towards them. He undid
the cinch on his saddle and grinned to himself. That boy
was a plumb magnet when it came to attracting young
females. He piled his saddle and sweaty blankets on the
ground and let Diablo go roll in the dust.

The mule unloaded, Slocum went back to the corral.
The three girls were seated on the ground in the shade
and watched things closely. Benny stood in the same place
and intently studied the horse and Baca's moves.

"Is he horse or devil?" Slocum asked.

"Pretty much horse," Benny said with a favorable grin
on his brown lips.

Baca soon had a saddle on the colt. Slocum could see
the horse listened to his every word. Quietly and softly,

Baca spoke to him in Spanish. There was no doubt that in less than a half hour, the youth had won the horse's confidence. He no longer acted compelled to strike or fear this "new thing" in his life.

In their colorful full skirts and blouses, the three girls seated on the ground watched with intensity. White girls the same age would have become bored and moved on, but Indian women appreciated man-animal relationships. Horses saved them the burden of bearing the camp goods on their backs when they moved. Many times the bucks left the details of the horses to the women. They were there for the lesson, and whispered quietly when he did something new with the watch-eyed mustang.

Slocum guessed the threesome to be close in age to the boy. His good looks added to their attraction; an occasional giggle told him enough about the situation. It wasn't all horse-training that drew them there.

Two hours later, Baca swung in the saddle and calmly rode the colt around the pen. A little uncertain in his gait, Watch-eye made a few rollers out his nostrils and settled in soon to a trot. Baca reined him with the bosal reins, and the girls nodded their impressed approval.

"What do you think now?" Slocum asked Benny.

"I think I should turn him loose."

"Why? Baca has him half broke for you."

"I still see spirits in his eyes."

"Do whatever you wish. Can you ride with us tomorrow up there?" Slocum asked with a nod toward the north.

"Sure," Benny said.

Baca came over and handed the reins to him.

"Damn, it is sure hot," the boy said, slicing the sweat off his forehead with his index finger.

"Go take a dip in the river," Slocum said. "We'll have something to eat about sundown."

"Anywhere along here?" Baca asked, motioning toward the river.

"Sure, Indians won't look," Slocum told him, then wondered if he had told the boy a lie. Those three curious girls might. Oh, hell, Baca knew what to do with them.

Slocum watched the boy, with his sombrero on his shoulder and raven black wavy hair glistening in the sun, head for the Verde. He even felt a twang of jealousy, but instead went with Benny to his wickiup.

Atockia, the woman who lived with Benny, was at least ten years younger than him. She came out at their approach, looked up, and grinned at Slocum. Except for the missing tip of her nose and the long-ago scarred tissue disfiguring her face, she would have been handsome. Slocum knew bucks used a knife to whittle on their women's noses whenever they suspected them of infidelity.

He once saw a beautiful Apache woman whose husband had cut the tendons at the ankle in one of her legs so she could not run away from him again. The poor girl was forced to crawl about camp.

Benny and Slocum retired to sit on a log in the shade.

"This fella Montrose got many with him?" Benny asked.

"Three to six."

"Three of us be enough?"

"I figure so. We take many more up there, he'll get wise to it and we won't surprise him."

Benny nodded and then grinned. "That boy as good with women as he is with horses?"

Slocum glanced toward the river and the towering rustling cottonwoods. Under them, the three girls busily undressed on the sandy bank. The shafts of sunlight reflected off their sleek copper-colored skin. Even at the distance, he could make out their shapely butts and firm pointed breasts.

"He better be," he said to Benny, and they both laughed.

21

The three of them rode north before dawn. After a late night out with his newfound girlfriends, Baca looked drawn and quartered to the amused Slocum. Little of the boy's usual youthful vigor was apparent when the gold orbit of the sun stole its way over Four Peaks. Baca brought on the mule, and they followed the road that Slocum knew would soon peter out into a single trail, beyond where the last Yavapia lived in a brush-canvas-covered structure that looked like a beehive.

Naked children played about their homes, and grew silent at the riders' approach. Standing almost at attention, they watched with dark curious eyes at the passage of the three men.

"You didn't turn the watch-eye loose today?" Slocum asked, curious about the scout's feeling toward the horse.

"I am still thinking about him," Benny said.

Slocum knew that was all the conversation he would get from the scout. He had heard the man tell his squaw to cut grass for them and water the two while he was gone. A chore she no doubt did all the time anyway, since that was women's work.

While they rode north, Slocum discussed with Benny

finding a way to get into the basin without Montrose learning that they were coming. To ride straight up the Verde would bring them to the same place where Slocum had been when Montrose forced him to go to his camp.

"We must cross the mountains and go in from over there," Benny said matter-of-factly.

Slocum studied the desert hills and agreed. If Benny knew a way, so much the better. He had to accept the man's word on it. Sometimes it was bad to assume things with Indians. Once, with the army in Mexico, following some tracks, Slocum had been certain the scout knew the country they were in—that he had been there before. It had turned out the Apache had never been close to the place in his entire life. He'd shrugged off Slocum's concern with: "They are only mountains, which lead to more mountains."

At midday, when they crossed through a giant malapia boulder-strewn pass and the hot south wind dried Slocum's sweaty face, he felt more certain that Benny did know the way. Below them more greasewood, green paloverde, and giant saguaros forested the desert. It was good to dismount, undo the cinch, let the horses rest, and empty his bladder.

"How far away are they?" Baca asked after taking a swig of water from his canteen and wiping his mouth on the back of his hand.

"One or two days' ride," Benny said.

The youth nodded, and looked out of squinted eyes at the wide valley beneath them.

"Sure glad you all drug me out of there."

"Ft. McDowell?" Slocum glanced over at him.

"Yeah, I don't think I could have done it one more time." He shook his head as if dismayed.

"You'll be surprised how fast you'll recover," Slocum said, and clapped him on the shoulder. Then both he and Benny laughed at Baca's expense.

•   •   •

By sundown, they'd reached a place where several springs pooled up in potholes. It was cooler up there, Slocum decided, than in the desert behind them. A few scrub junipers began to dot the hillsides. Benny said they should make camp there, that the sun was low enough in the west.

Baca gathered firewood and put on a pot of frijoles. Slocum reset a loose shoe on the boy's horse, and Benny rested with his back to a boulder. Twilight set in before they tried the beans and decided to eat them.

"How much further?" Slocum asked, seated cross-legged with the fire's radiant heat reflecting on his face.

"There is a spring if it hasn't gone dry we can camp at," said Benny. "If Montrose is in that canyon you told me about, it is only a few miles away from there."

"He's like a bear. I figure he's denned up there or will return there."

Benny nodded between spoonfuls of beans. The frijoles weren't that good-tasting to Slocum, and the scout must be starved. Poor Baca was about to fall asleep eating.

They soon climbed in their bedrolls to the lullaby of coyotes. Their mournful wails filled the starlighted night, and gave Slocum plenty of time to think about his plans for taking Montrose.

First, he needed to separate the leader from his gang. One by one, he wanted to drive off his helpers, and then settle with the big man alone. How to do it still eluded him. Something would work out. He thought about Maria, her supple body like silk against him. Damn, just the notion of her made him hard. He'd been a damn fool to ride off and leave a woman as passionate as her. He closed his eyes to the steel facts of reality—no way he could have stayed at her hacienda any longer. The realization of his loss caused a ball to form in his stomach; he finally went to sleep.

• • •

At sunup, they rode north into Bloody Basin. The junipers grew taller, and the grass too. It was a vast rolling land of canyons and hills that drew its name from the vicious Apache raids in times past upon the ranchers who'd tried to stock it with cattle and make their home in it.

The spring the Indian led them to proved strong, and Benny nodded his approval when they reached it. He only dismounted long enough to water his horse, then remounted and told Slocum he would scout the outlaws and be back.

Giving the man his blessings, Slocum and Baca unloaded. They set up a canvas fly for shade on a flat spot above the spring. Then Baca went for wood. Slocum didn't want much fire. At times wood smoke could be smelled at great distances, and he wanted nothing to alert the outlaws.

He made a small cooking fire in a hole under the beans and let them cook. With the stock hobbled and with plenty of graze, he waited for the return of the Yavapia. Baca took the opportunity for another siesta.

The scout returned at dusky dark. Slocum was anxious to hear the man's words, and filled a coffee cup and a tin plate heaping with beans for the scout. He'd put too much dried chili in this kettle, but Benny would never notice. Both Slocum and the boy waited for the scout's report.

"Four in camp. Counting Montrose." Benny busied himself eating.

"Two are Baca's age?" Slocum asked.

Benny nodded, his mouth full.

"Then the other must be Wilton, he's older."

"Yeah."

"Any idea how to separate them?"

Benny grinned and nodded. "Let me sneak up and put a stick of dynamite in one's bedroll and light the fuse. That will scare them, huh?"

"Too dangerous. They might shoot you in the process. They will ride out sooner or later for supplies or to kill another calf. When they come back, I want to have dynamite set up to go off all over their camp and we'll have us a Fourth of July."

"Then what?" Baca asked.

"When they get confused enough, we'll take them. What do you think, Benny?"

"Sounds like gawdamn fun." Then he laughed.

"We start spying on them tomorrow," Slocum said. "We'll take turns watching them and when they ride out, we set the dynamite and wait for their return."

"What if they leave for good?" Baca asked.

"No, they are wanted in too many places to leave a good thing. They will make some raids, but this fortress is near impenetrable and beyond the reach of most lawmen to come up here looking for them. Montrose has his bluff in on everyone else up here too."

Days dragged on. The three men each took turns spying on the outlaws. Montrose stayed close to his camp. Slocum did his guard duty on top of the high bluff and out of sight, and could hear the outlaw's raspy voice cursing and shouting at times as well as if he were right in camp with him.

Then a phrase slipped out. "Black Canyon stage." Slocum smiled and rubbed his beard-stubbled cheek. At last they were going off to do something criminal that would require them to leave the hideout.

Shortly after the outlaws cleared the camp, Slocum and his two men rode in. Dynamite was buried in shallow holes and the fuses disguised under grass clippings. Then they worked along the trail, setting charges in the junipers beside it. His plan was to chase the outlaws into their camp and so disorganize them, they would surrender. And if they wouldn't give up, he planned to blow them up.

"It isn't all pretty women," Slocum said, overseeing Baca's work to wrap and tie the red stick to the trunk of the juniper. "You bored yet?"

"It has been slow, but I am feeling better now."

"They may not come back," Slocum said to warn him. The boy blinked at him.

"Naw, they'll be back, but I am not certain when," Slocum added. "We won't use all our dynamite to drive them in. Save some to dissuade them if they decide to run for it."

"Good idea. What's Benny doing?" Baca asked, searching around.

"Using some greasewood to brush out our tracks so the outlaws don't see them and get jumpy."

"Good idea." Baca finished knotting the sisal rope around the stick, and cut off the excess.

They waited nearly two days for the gang's return. Hours dragged by without a breeze to stir the oven-hot air. Sick of cold half-cooked frijoles and canteen water, at the sounds of the outlaws' horses returning, Slocum sent off his helpers to take their places.

Then came the creak of saddle leather, and Slocum could visualize the burly outlaw in the lead. He recognized the half-Percheron horse's loud breathing and snorting. Slocum counted the horses going past. When the last one went by, he lit his fuses, and then hurried to creep closer before the charges went off behind the gang.

He ducked down and covered his ears at the last minute. The explosions blew dust, tree limbs, and cedar boughs into the air.

"It's a trap!" Montrose shouted, and as Slocum had figured, the outlaws started out of the canyon. The blast set off by Benny drove billowing clouds of dirt in the air and cut off any escape. Instead they charged back into their camp.

Slocum, with his rifle in his hand, hurried to the rise to see the outlaws dismounting from their wide-eyed horses in a confusion he wanted to prolong.

"Throw down your arms or die!" Slocum shouted, and quickly ducked down, drawing the pistol shots of the angry gang members. He could hear the unmistakable voice of Montrose cussing his lineage and ancestors above all of it.

"Your funeral," he said to himself. The blast of the dynamite charges around the camp set off by Baca sent the panic-stricken horses tearing away. Slocum could see the gang members, hands held high, stumbling out of the cloud of dust that rose as high as the tree tops. Only three. Where was Montrose? Slocum searched for him among the others.

"I'm going to kill you!" Montrose roared, and with both pistols drawn, came staggering into view.

"Put them down," Slocum ordered. His finger itched on the trigger.

"You son of a bitch, it's you, Slocum!"

"Drop the guns or die, Montrose."

"Go to hell!"

The report of the rifle shattered the canyon. It echoed and re-echoed off the towering stone faces. Pitching forward, Montrose fired one bullet in the dust, then fell facedown. Baca stepped forward in his once-white clothing now brown with dirt, and held the smoking rifle, looking at the still form on the ground.

"You did the right thing," Slocum said to reassure the boy. "It was him or us."

Unceremoniously, Benny brought a camp ax and with four or five overhead whacks, decapitated the outlaw's head. He put the bloody trophy in a gunnysack, while the shocked surviving outlaws stood with their hands high, pale-faced, and watched the entire operation.

"That's good for much money," Benny said, holding the bag up.

"You boys get the idea?" Slocum asked, herding the prisoners to a place away from their gear and possible weapons. They only grumbled to themselves. He thought they said something about "the damn bloodthirsty Indian."

"What should we do next?" Baca asked with the prisoners bound up for the night.

"You and Benny need to take them and Montrose's head to Prescott and collect the rewards. Should make you two pretty rich."

"Why won't you go with us?" Baca asked.

"I've got places to be. You two can handle getting them there."

"But I kinda like riding with you."

"You're a good man to ride with, Baca. But my trails are too long and hard for a man without a wanted poster on him to have to endure."

"Will you come back by the hacienda again?" Baca asked.

"I doubt it."

"Maria will miss you."

"I'll miss her too." He studied the youth. Good man. He had sure never complained a minute while waiting for their chance to take the outlaws.

"Tell her Montrose is dead and won't ever bother her again."

"She will be relieved."

Slocum agreed and tightened his cinch.

"Thanks," he said quietly to both men. Then he shook their hands and rode out.

"Come by Ft. McDowell, I'll give you a good horse next time," Benny shouted after him. Slocum threw him a wave and in the growing twilight, rode out of the canyon.

• • •

A month later, in Socorro, New Mexico Territory, Slocum read the Sante Fe newspaper. The headline spelled it out: THREE GANG MEMBERS HUNG BY ARIZONA SHERIFF. The remaining outlaws had been executed by Sheriff T. J. Goodwin for the robbery of the Black Canyon stage and the murder of its guard.

Seated on top of the homemade quilt with his back to the iron headboard, Slocum looked up when Ivy Muldoone swept in the room. Dressed in her best blue outfit, which tightly fit her curvaceous body, she looked perturbed.

"What's wrong?" he asked, looking up from a second article. It told of the marriage of Captain Igor Bollinsky, in charge of the State of Sonora's *rurales,* to hacienda owner Maria Cardinale Obregon. The best man had been Baca Delone.

"There's a gawdamn blanket-ass Appaloosa horse down the street at the hitch rack in front of the Red Bucket Saloon," Ivy said. With impatience written on her handsome face, she began undoing the buttons down the front of her dress.

"Abbott brothers are here already?" he asked, pained at her words.

"It ain't the damn Nez Percé Indians. I went down and checked. It's them two, all right, but they never saw me. They arrived in town a half hour ago."

"Don't leave us much time, does it?" he asked.

"I know. I know. That's why I'm hurrying so. Oh! Help me get out of this damn thing," she said, already down to her stark white corset. "Unbutton it."